METH, COL'AN
and other
theologians

Also by Clifford Meth

FICTION & VERSE:
   girl (1983)
   Crib Death & Other Bedtime Stories (1995)
   This Bastard Planet (1995)
   The White Man Dancing (1996)
   Crawling From the Wreckage (The White Man Limping) (1996)
   Perverts, Pedophiles & Other Theologians (1997)
   Crib Death: The Baby-sitter's Companion (1997)
   Conflicts of Disinterest (1998)
   Wearing The Horns (2003)
   god's 15 minutes (2004)
   The Three Tenors: Off key
      (with Dave Cockrum & Wm. Messner-Loebs) (2005)
   MethO.D. (2006)
   One Small Voice (2008)

GRAPHIC NOVELS:
   Snaked (2008)

AS EDITOR:
   Strange Kaddish (1996)
   Stranger Kaddish (1997)
   The Graveyards are Filled with Dead Heroes (1997)
   The Uncanny Dave Cockrum Tribute (2004)
   Heroes and Villains (with Neal Adams) (2005)
   Balm in Gilead (2007)

METH, COL'AN
and other theologians

HANK MAGITZ
ADAM AUSTIN
STEVE GERBER
MARV WOLFMAN
MARK EVANIER
GAIL SIMONE

All stories copyright © 2008 by Clifford Meth

Published by Aardwolf Publishing, 179-9 Rt. 46 West, Box 252, Rockaway, NJ 07866 U.S.A.; email sales@aardwolfpublishing.com

All rights reserved. All wrongs reversed. No part of this book may be reproduced without written permission from the author or his authorized agent. All stories in this book are works of fiction. Names, characters, places and incidents are either products of the author's imagination or are used fictitiously, more or less. The stories contained in this book first appeared in *Perverts, Pedophiles & Other Theologians* (copyright © 1997 by Clifford Meth), except for "Economics 101" and "Scary Faces" which appear for the first time in this publication. All of the stories included in this volume have been revised and are the author's preferred text.

All forwards, afterwords, intermissions or any manner of essays by writers other than Clifford Meth are used with permission and are copyrights of their respective authors.

Cover art: Background art copyright © 2008 by Mark Staff Brandl; illustration © 1997 Gene Colan and Jeff Amano
All interior illustrations (except for doodles by Mike Lily and Mike Pascale) are copyright © Gene Colan and are used by permission.
Daredevil is a TM of Marvel Entertainment.

Book design by Richard Sheinaus

First printed in The United States of America, 2008
Regular edition ISBN 978-1-888669-16-9
Signed/numbered edition ISBN 978-1-888669-17-6

Printed in the United States by Morris Publishing
3212 East Highway 30
Kearney, NE 68847
1-800-650-7888

*For three decades of Friendship
where all roads have led to Rockaway,
this one is for
David Michael Vnenchak*

PART ZERO

MUCH ADO

FOREWORD:
WHEN WORLDS COLLIDE

When I sit to compose a few words about Clifford Meth, I find myself envying people like Wm. Messner-Loebs, Marv Wolfman and Peter David—writers who, because of their casual acquaintanceship with Cliff, are comfortable painting him from a finite palette. In his afterword to Meth's *One Small Voice*, Loebs describes Meth as "artistically erotic" while Peter David opens *MethO.D.* by calling attention to the disquieting dark side of Meth's prose. Harlan Ellison, as only Harlan Ellison can, depicts the rarified components of Meth's Arthurian loyalty in his afterword to *god's 15 minutes* whereas Mark Evanier and Gail Simone, in this volume, discuss a kinder, gentler Meth.

All true, but none of these descriptions, taken alone, adequately portray the complex man that I've shared a friendship and a publishing relationship with for two decades. It reminds me of the parable of the six blind men who each mis-describe an elephant based on their own limited physical examinations of its singular body parts: the trunk, the tusk, the tail, the underbelly...

No one does justice to Meth—the writer, the friend, the performance artist, the *force*—with a several-hundred word essay because Clifford cannot be understood without accepting the contradictions. Only an *unorthodox* Jew, as he has described himself, could embrace the philosophies of John Lennon and Meir Kahane at the same time. The longer you know him, the more the paradoxes add up. On a personal front, Cliff's reclusive nature stands in sharp contrast with his charisma; watching him command an audience, you'd never guess his dread of crowds. His stories, though laden with biographical elements, display the rare quality of having been written by someone who is dedicated to *story*. The play is the thing and Meth understands this; he is both actor and audience, an artist who embodied gonzo journalism at its primal level then ate from the tree of fiction and found himself liberated from the garden.

"Meth is a dangerous writer," said artist Neal Adams. "He doesn't seem to care if you like him." Also true: Cliff writes for Cliff…that is, *when* he writes. Unlike the young songwriter I knew in the late 80s, middle-aged Meth must frequently be steered back to the typewriter else he finds himself escaping the call. The truth is he would prefer getting into a fight; he knows he can win at

FOREWORD

that game. Writing, on the other hand, seems to scare him, as it would anyone so self-flagellating.

In another corner, Cliff embodies self-sacrifice, continually proving himself a dedicated friend to writers and artists of previous generations who did not receive their fair share of the pie. His crusades on behalf of certain creators have brought him more than his fair share of fame bytes in the comics community, but this persona is no more real than the dark poet who writes of whorehouses and drunken brawls with the resonance of experience. The multitudes are real and they are not done with bravado but abandon. Cliff is unaware of the sidelines, but in contrast to his reality, the stories that emerge from him are often escapist. As one reviewer put it, "If Kurt Vonnegut and Flannery O'Conner made a baby and allowed Quentin Tarantino to raise it, you'd have Clifford Meth."

What a formidable combination, marrying Meth's expansive personality and unique voice to the inimitable art talent of Gene Colan. What a pleasure publishing this team once again!

— Jim Reeber
July 2008
Rockaway, New Jersey

INTRODUCTION:
Delve Into the Dark Side

When asked to write a new introduction to this book, I wasn't sure I knew what to say. I'd only read some of Clifford Meth's work, and the material I *had* read was incredibly dark, even for someone like me who enjoys writing dark stories. But the stories were illustrated by Gene Colan and I knew Gene's work *really* well, first as a fan, then as a collaborator on a large number of comics over a long, long period of time. Over 35 years, actually.

I first saw Gene's work in the Warren magazines. They were magnificently rendered B&W stories with tones of gray. Back then, Warren published work by some of the most amazing artists who had ever been involved with comics, from Frank Frazetta and Al Williamson to Reed Crandall and Gray Morrow. These were all people whose work I had grown up buying, and though I had never seen Gene's work before that I was aware of (because most comics were uncredited back then), his art belonged next to all these legends. What I immediately noticed was that Gene drew people and not cartoons. His figures looked like people you would see walking down the street; they had lives and they had flesh and bone and they weren't merely line drawings. In a world where so many cartoonists had similar styles, Gene's art stood apart.

I continued to be a fan of Gene's work, but then something happened. I had been writing "mystery" stories for DC Comics for a year or two. Mysteries were what we called the watered-down horror stories that comics were doing in lieu of real horror stories, which were then forbidden by the Comics Code. They were usually little shock stories with O'Henry-like twist endings. I wrote a number of them when Roy Thomas asked me to send Marvel some ideas for their brand new mystery book, *Tower of Shadows*. Somehow I sold one, and lo and behold my very first Marvel story was drawn by Gene! I couldn't have been happier.

Soon after, Gene was drawing a new book for Marvel entitled *The Tomb of Dracula*. This was a revolutionary comic in several ways. Stan Lee had been pushing the Comics Code to change and for the first time in nearly two decades comics could again feature such classic characters as vampires and werewolves—creatures and concepts that had been removed from comics

INTRODUCTION

since the frightening witch-hunt days of Frederick Wertham. Secondly, *ToD* was the first new continuing comic to feature a villain as the protagonist. Writer Gerry Conway wrote the first two issues, Archie Goodwin wrote issues 3 & 4, and Gardner Fox penned issues 5 & 6—but they were all drawn by Gene who, because of his love of the old black and white Universal films, very much wanted to draw the book (which had initially been assigned to George Tuska). Gene actually auditioned for the job, something that someone of his tenure at Marvel didn't need to do. The result: Stan Lee loved what he saw and Gene got the job and George, an incredibly talented artist in his own right, received a different project.

Having three writers in six issues was not a good beginning so when Roy asked me if I wanted to be writer #4, I wasn't all that anxious to do it. But Gene was drawing the book so I said yes. Then Gene and I went on to do 63 more issues until its voluntary end with issue #70. The only reason we ended the book was that after more than eight years Gene wanted to move onto different projects, and I didn't want to do the book with anyone but him.

Over time, Gene and I created characters like Hannibal King and Deacon Frost who made it into film. And there was also our character Blade, which went on to three major motion pictures and a TV series.

As a comics writer one of the things you worry about most is how the story will look once it's drawn. Will the artist tell the story you've asked him to tell or will he change it for the worse? Will the artist understand what you're asking for and make your idea come alive or will he or she bury it? With Gene you never had to worry. Whatever you gave him to draw came back better than you could have imagined.

Going back to this introduction, I knew I could write about Gene's art because I loved it, but I wasn't sure about the stories. If I was going to say something in print, I had to really like what I read... Fortunately, Clifford didn't make that difficult! His writing is dark, relentless and always in your face. It doesn't make for easy reading because it is highly emotional and forces you to pay attention, but that is the best thing a writer can do. We often read Teflon stories where your eyes glide over the words and you come out smiling but that's all. There's nothing to root on or remember. Meth's work is quite the opposite; it *always* challenges you. He doesn't hold back and he doesn't let you pay half attention. You might even turn away from some of his twistier concepts, but I don't think he expects otherwise. Clifford Meth writes from a place others won't walk.

Perverts, Pedophiles & Other Theologians, filled with darkness and blank verse, will assault you with its chilling imagery. These stories force you into some queasy speculations that make everything you read even creepier. You'll find Clifford's strength is that he makes your imagination work overtime… again, it's one of the best things a writer can do.

— Marv Wolfman
June 2008
Los Angeles, California

ORIGINAL FOREWORD:
Writing Pains

When I asked Clifford Meth what sort of introduction he'd like for *Perverts, Pedophiles and Other Theologians*, he replied: "Whatever you want." Big help.

Well, the introduction should be about you and Gene Colan, I said.

"I don't want to read a lot of praise about me," Cliff said (at which point, of course, I was tempted to ask who said anything about praise?) "Why don't you talk about the pain of writing or something?"

Okay. Fine. The Pain of Writing.

In a moment.

First, though, a few words about Clifford Meth and Gene Colan.

Cliff and I have never met. The sum total of our personal interaction consists of a few e-mails, a couple of phone calls, and the manuscript material he sent me to read. I have learned, however, that he spends his days as a technical writer, despite a pronounced aversion to anything technical; that he respects and admires many of the same science-fiction writers and comic book creators that I do; that he met on at least one occasion The Lubavitcher Rebbe; and, based on the aforementioned manuscript, that he writes very well about very intimate subjects.

Gene Colan and I have met, though not as often as you might expect for two people who've collaborated so frequently in comics. Gene was the regular artist on *Howard the Duck*, a character I created and wrote for Marvel Comics. He drew *Stewart the Rat*, my first graphic novel. He illustrated *The Phantom Zone*, a Superman mini-series I wrote for DC Comics. And over the years, we've probably done a couple of dozen more stories together—Dracula trapped in the Vatican and the 100th issue of *Daredevil* (in which Marvel's Man Without Fear was interviewed by Jann Wenner, the publisher of *Rolling Stone*) come to mind immediately.

I can truthfully say that there's no artist I've enjoyed working with more. Unlike far too many comic book artists who simply draw big guys in spandex with bulging muscles, Gene draws characters. He imbues his people with a quality of portraiture that I've never seen duplicated by another comics artist, and, even more remarkably, he accomplishes it without sacrificing the energy and consistency so necessary to telling a story in a sequence of panels.

I could go on and on about the cinematic nature of his work, the way he uses light and shadow to evoke a mood, the verisimilitude with which he rendered a cartoon duck and a genetically engineered rat, or the flesh-and-blood humanity he brought to *Superman*—but it's probably best that I stop blathering and allow you to experience Gene for yourself.

Besides, I have to discuss The Pain of Writing, remember?

Here's a little secret that writers don't usually care to reveal: When the work is going well, the pain is minimal. The words pour out, the images flow, and it's almost like watching a show play itself out on the paper or computer screen. It's not just painless, it's actually fun.

Here's another little secret that writers don't usually care to reveal: When the words won't come, when the images don't coalesce, when the actors in the show keep muffing their lines despite the writer's best efforts, the pain is damn near indescribable. When you care about the work, it's even worse—like drilling down into the depths of your soul without anesthetic and coming up with a bucket full of sludge. I don't know if this happens to every writer, but it's happened to me. And it's torture.

A friend of mine once described the act of writing as routinely making something out of nothing. Never mind bricks without straw. We're talking bricks without clay. A mind, ten fingers, a keyboard, and a blank sheet of paper or a terrifyingly white screen—these are the only raw materials a writer has to work with. Somehow, the neurons have to fire in such a way that when the fingers strike the keyboard, the little black marks that appear on the page or on screen will combine to comprise a cast of characters, the words they speak, the places they inhabit, indeed the totality of their lives.

When I think about this, when I stop to consider that it's how I've chosen to earn my livelihood, I fear a little for my sanity and wonder if I wouldn't be happier selling shoes.

You know something? I probably would.

ORIGINAL FOREWORD

But I would never have had the opportunity to work with Gene Colan (unless my shoe store happened to be located in his neighborhood), and I would never have been asked to write the introduction to this book—in which case you might have gone through life believing that the only pain associated with writing was the result of carpal tunnel syndrome.

Worse yet, imagine if Clifford Meth had opted for exploring your sole rather than his soul. This book might not exist, and you'd be deprived of some very thoughtful prose and poetry.

Put those pumps back in the stock room and clock me out. Bring on the perverts, pedophiles, and the rest of God's children.

— Steve Gerber
March 1997
Burbank, California

ORIGINAL INTRODUCTION:
TESTOSTERONE, ADRENALINE & A LITTLE MARIJUANA

"It doesn't need an introduction," I told Jim Reeber, my editor. "The stories speak for themselves." But he knew I was just being lazy (read: I had nothing to say). That I'd walk around like that for days, perhaps weeks, until something leaped out.

And then Bob Kroenke died.

Kroenke wasn't a guy I'd ever mentioned in a story. We'd never gotten drunk together nor fought our way out of a whorehouse. Nothing that romantic. Just a hard-working, straight-shooting, ex-hippy I'd worked with back when I was with *Electronic Design*; a good guy who hadn't given up the cigarettes or the ponytail or the attitude. It's all in the attitude.

I write about things that move me; things I find funny or pathetic. You might have read some of it. I don't write much about my wife because she's normal and healthy and she smells clean, and my characters (the people I find funny and pathetic) are base and foul and beautiful losers. Like the rest of us.

Like Bob Kroenke. Dead at 44. An aneurysm in the middle of the day. His little daughter found him stretched out in the middle of the bathroom.

It made me somber. Made me pick up the phone and call old friends to make sure they were still alive, and that I hadn't forgotten to tell them I love them.

I don't think I loved Bob Kroenke. I love him now that he's dead. Everybody does that. Six feet down, they love you to pieces. Good old Kroenke. Always positive. Always there with a smile and a pat on the back, asking about my next book, though he hadn't read the last one yet. A good fellow. I can see him now in those jeans and old Keds, slouching from the weight of the 10,000 lbs. of shit he shouldered—an ex-wife, the IRS, life's little tears; standing outside in the warm sun and sucking down cigarettes like there was no tomorrow, which there wasn't.

I could have called this book "Testosterone, Adrenaline & a little Marijuana." It's about the people I know, regular people, all the assholes in the world and mine.

ORIGINAL INTRODUCTION

Beautiful losers. Just like the rest of us. Here today. Gone tomorrow.

There's a lesson in that, for me anyway: If you have something to say, say it. Smoke 'em if you've got em. After adolescence, it goes pretty fast.

— Clifford Meth
March 1997
Rockaway, New Jersey

PART ONE

OVER-
TURE

DEEP KIMCHEE

So Dave was out of work again, which was nobody's fault but just the way the world seemed to function, guys like Dave, good hard-working sons of bitches looking for work and pinkie-ringed, glad-handed, ass-licking dickboys driving around in new Mercedes. God invented flies, too. Why complain about it? And Dave wasn't complaining, just looking for work and doing odd jobs to make ends meet. Like this one. Asked Hank to type his résumé and a couple cover letters. That's what happens to the world's great poets. People give them résumés to type. But Hank wasn't complaining, either.

Dave dropped by around noon. Hank stopped typing, went to the refrigerator and took out the corned beef sandwich he'd made the night before. Three-day-old corned beef is better than no corned beef. he offered to make Dave a sandwich but Dave said he wasn't hungry. He was smoking Winstons, lit another one and said, "if something doesn't happen soon, I'm in deep *kimchee*."

"What's *kimchee*?" asked Hank, his mouth full of corned beef.

"A Korean delicacy. Saw it when I was stationed near Pohang, a village in South Korea less than a mile from the DMZ. They take raw cabbage and eggs and bury it underground for six months in a sealed clay pot so it can ferment. Then they dig it up. If you had one here, they could smell it over in Boonton."

"You ate that shit?"

"Not me. I've eaten lots of nasty things, but not *kimchee*. Got beer?"

"Sure."

Hank got two beers, finished half his sandwich, wrapped the other half up in a paper napkin and stuck it in his pocket. Then he and Dave left the apartment and got into Hank's car, which Dave had borrowed earlier that morning. Dave threw Hank the keys.

"It's in the trunk?" asked Hank.

"It's in the trunk," said Dave.

They drove toward Rockaway. it was about a 20-minute ride. To anyone not from there, Rockaway was just another jerkwater town. To Hank and Dave, it was home. Better than home. Street Eden.

"I've been thinking about going back to Morris Hills," said Hank. "Haven't been there twice since we graduated. I want to see the old teachers, see if any of them are left." he realized it had been 17 years. The old teachers were probably dead by now. Dead or dying. "I bet Miss DeSota is still there."

"I remember her," said Dave. "Guidance counselor."

"Whatever *that* means." Hank scratched his ass. "Remember Mrs. Laflamme, the English teacher?"

"Yeah."

"Bet she's still there, too. Now there was a good teacher. I always wanted to fuck her."

"You should have."

"Should have but didn't. Maybe I ought to go there now and tell her, hey, Mrs. Laflamme, remember me? I always wanted to fuck you." He thought about that for a minute. "She was like 35 then. That would make her 52 now."

"Nasty," said Dave. "You'd have to use a hose to get her wet."

"Jeezus, 52," said Hank. "I don't ever want to get that old."

The two pulled off the highway and took the back roads into Rockaway, passed the park, the Catholic high school and cemetery, then turned down Greenpond Road and headed toward Split Rock. Around the bend, Wildcat Mountain suddenly came into view. "Seems like they've been building that golf course forever," said Hank.

"What golf course?"

"That Arnold Palmer's."

"Gave up on that two years ago," said Dave. He struck a match, lit another cigarette. "Town wouldn't let them finish. Some politician didn't get greased. Take a look at that gouge."

Hank turned to look as they passed the mountain. a crevice had been cut through the trees, but the path was already overgrown. it was a good sight. "Good," he said. "Fuck 'em with their stupid golf courses." there were few things Hank could think of stupider than golf. Video games, maybe.

Finally, the two reached Split Rock. it was a great, wide reservoir, hidden by thick, high trees, lush foliage and very few houses. The entire area was posted NO HUNTING, NO FISHING, NO WOOD CHOPPING, NO TRESPASSING. It was a very quiet place where nothing ever seemed to happen, except every once in a while a body would pop out of the water, usually decomposed and half eaten by fish. It was a great place to dump a body if you killed someone.

Hank parked the car, then the two got out and walked. The rocks were slippery and moss covered. There was poison ivy everywhere. They saw a deer and a few snake holes, but no snakes. Satisfied that the area was clear, they went back to the car and opened the trunk, then lifted out the sack, two shovels, and a bag of lime, then carried them down the hill toward the water.

"Heavy," said Hank.

"*Fucking* heavy," said Dave.

They dug a hole, dumped the sack, added lime, then filled in the hole. The whole thing took about 30 minutes.

"You hungry yet?" Hank asked once he was back in the car.

"Nope," said Dave. "I never eat lunch."

"Big breakfast?"

"Never eat breakfast, either." Dave lit a cigarette.

Hank unwrapped his half sandwich, took a big bite of bread and three-day-old corned beef, barely chewed it, swallowed. "When the fuck *do* you eat?"

"At night." Dave puffed out blue-white smoke, huge rings, like a diesel showing off. "I eat a big dinner. Keeps me going all day."

As Hank drove out of Split Rock, Dave pointed out various spots, boyhood memories, places he hiked as a Boy Scout, fishing holes, the first place he ever got tit. "See that? The Flying Dutchman?" He aimed his finger at the outside of the tavern. It was in terrible shape—busted screen door, fallen shudders. "One time," said Dave, "I pulled in there with my old man. He told me to wait in the car and he went in for a six-pack. A minute later, this guy comes flying out the door, blood coming out of his eye. My father punched him right through the door."

"Why?" asked Hank.

"Fucked if I know. The old man just got back in with his six-pack and drove off."

Suddenly, Hank put the pedal to the floor and the car jerked forward.

"What's wrong?" asked Dave.

"I've got to take a dump!" Hank kept the pedal down, drove like a lunatic around the winding roads and almost hit a tree.

"Better slow the fuck down before a cop pulls us over."

"Can't," said Hank. "I really have to shit!"

"So pull over and shit!" said Dave.

"I don't have any fucking toilet paper! Used to carry an emergency roll in the trunk. Why the fuck did I stop doing that?" Hank sped up. "Jesus Murphy—I have to GO."

"Use leaves," said Dave.

"I've got hemorrhoids," said Hank. "You know what fucking leaves feel like on fucking hemorrhoids?"

"Nasty," said Dave. "So just hold it in. It's all in your mind. I can go two, three days without taking a shit. Went four days once."

"Four days?"

"Yup."

"I'd fucking die. They'd find me on the side of the road with shit coming out of my ears. Four days! Christ."

"It's all in your head."

"Like hell. I respect you and all, Dave, but I have to disagree on this one. My brain bone is not connected to my assbone or my bowels or whatever the fuck. When I have to shit, I *have* to shit. No arguments. I get up in the morning, man, I take three shits before I even leave the apartment. The first shit is just to get the machine moving. Then there's the real shit, the *big* shit. Then, maybe ten minutes later, there's one more—the *after* shit. And that's before I even have a coffee."

"You're just full of shit," said Dave.

"Yeah, well maybe if you'd fucking eat something instead of sucking cigarettes all day, you'd shit, too. Besides, shitting is one of life's great pleasures. There's eating and there's shitting. Why deny yourself that?"

Dave blew out puffs of smoke, cool as a stiff. "Just slow down," he said.

Twenty minutes later, they were back at Hank's apartment. Dave peeled the plastic off another box of Winstons, tapped it against his hand to pack down the tobacco, withdrew one, lit it, and inhaled deeply, like the smoke was good and clean and fresh. It's amazing what the body will get used to. And what the body wouldn't. Hank, for instance, was grunting audibly in the bathroom. To some people, hemorrhoids are worse than cancer. "You all right in there?" Dave asked.

"Fuck no," said Hank.

"Thought you said shitting was a pleasure."

There was the sound of a toilet flushing and then the door opened. "It is," said Hank. "It's *wiping* that's miserable."

"Thanks for sharing that."

Hank went to the fridge and got two beers, cracked one open, placed the other in front of Dave. "When do you think they'll find the body?"

Dave shrugged. "In the spring, probably. After the thaw. Some asshole will be out hunting and his dog will smell it."

"That's gotta smell nasty," said Hank. He pulled on his beer.

"No worse than *kimchee*," said Dave.

"Which is where I came in," said Hank, and he went back to his typewriter.

WHAT THEY DON'T KNOW

Roger H. sat impatiently in the reception area, filling out the job application with a Number Two pencil. Yes, he was a citizen. No, he didn't smoke. He paused at the last question.

Were you ever convicted of a felony?

He chuckled, wondered why a funeral parlor would care about that—as if someone might steal a body or something. No, he checked with conviction. No, he'd never been convicted. He stood up to deliver his application to the receptionist, which he'd been looking forward to for the last ten minutes.

Slumped in a swivel stool behind the glass, Carol Shuftan took a sip of her Diet Coke, then returned to buffing her just-polished nails. The young beauty had emerald-green eyes, full pouty lips and startling red hair bobbed like Hillary Clinton. She wore a white lambswool turtleneck tucked into a short tweed skirt, and black mesh stockings, which showed off pretty legs crossed neatly at the calf.

Roger's eyes were pinned to her legs, and then to her eyes, which flashed annoyance at his prolonged gape. He didn't read the look right, though, and was about to attempt conversation when the outside door popped open and in walked a tall, clean-shaven blond man in his early twenties, wearing a muscle shirt and a gold hoop in his right ear. He edged up alongside Roger at the window and asked for an application, then turned to Roger and winked.

Fucking queer, Roger thought.

***

"Did you get the job?"

"I got the job."

"Way to go, Rog!" said Al. Al was Roger's younger brother.

Roger took a short drag on his Marlboro. "I mean, how tough can it be? Eight bucks an hour to watch bodies at night. Like one's gonna get up and walk away."

"Sweet deal," said Al.

"And you should see the fringe benefits." Roger smirked.

"Like?"

"Like this receptionist. Unbelievable."

"Uh oh. Here he goes again."

"No," said Roger, "Really. This one's classy. And tits! D cups. No question."

"Yeah?"

"At least. But that don't make her a bad person, right?" Roger took another drag of his cigarette, then snuffed it in the kitchen sink. The butt fell beneath a pile of dirty dishes. "Can't wait to score her."

"Right," said Al. "Like you have a chance with an upscale broad."

"Fuck you, upscale. Betcha she's never been done right in her entire life. One look and I knew that. Nobody's ever satisfied that—not like I could."

"Listen to you."

"That's why I feel sorry for women," Roger said. "I mean, most guys aren't fulfilled because they're geeks. But women are unfulfilled because their *men* are geeks. It's wrong. Women get the shaft. They're like an oppressed minority. It's not even right to call them women any more. We should call them Female Americans."

***

Roger reported to work every night at ten minutes to ten, then he was out by 6 a.m. when the old groundskeeper opened up. Everyone who had ever worked for Young's Funeral Parlor agreed that it wasn't a bad job, as long as you didn't get spooked. And nothing spooked Roger. Not even when he was mopping up one night and a corpse moaned. He nearly laughed himself sick when another one farted.

"I smelled that, you bastard," he said. "What crawled up your ass and died?"

Roger often talked to the corpses. Eight hours is a long time to go without talking. So he talked to everything: the alley cats, the plants—even the huge picture in the vestibule of Jeremiah Young. Jeremiah had founded the funeral home in 1879.

"Smart move, Jerry." Roger pushed his mop passed the old portrait. "You found a trade that couldn't go out of business. Pretty sly," he said, ringing out his mop. "You son of a bitch."

Eventually, his rounds brought him to the reception area. The routine was always the same: He'd fill his bucket with hot water and detergent, then, before swabbing the black marble floor, he'd pause at the reception desk.

"And just what are we up to tonight, Miss Shuftan?" he asked her swivel chair. "Watching Letterman? Eating nachos? Greasing up the old vibrator?" Roger laughed. "Can't fool me, girl."

He slid open the top drawer of her desk. Carefully, he picked through the papers and pencils and Post-its and thumb tacks as he'd done every night since he began working. He didn't really know what he was searching for—anything personal of hers would have satisfied his curiosity. But the redhead left nothing behind. Even her desk blotter was vacant of personal items. The closest he got was a long-necked, empty bottle of Diet Coke.

"Is that a pubic hair on my Coke?" he asked in his best minstrel voice. He tossed the bottle into the trash.

Roger heard a key in the front door. He looked at his watch. 5:58 a.m. The groundskeeper walked in and locked the big oak door behind himself.

"Mornin', Rog."

"Hey, Jody."

The old man took several slow steps, smiled a pleasant smile. "How'd it go last night?"

"One of the stiff's farted in my general direction," said Roger.

"Hah!" The old man laughed. "They do that all th' time."

"Yeah, well I wasn't gonna take that crap from anyone."

The old man laughed again. "So whatcha do, huh?"

"Slapped him in the head, that's what. Teach 'em some respect for the living."

"Good for you," said Old Jody. He watched Roger make a fresh pot of coffee, scratched his face, warned Roger not use the milk, which had been sitting in the fridge for two weeks, and not to use the steps out back—said the wood was rotting through and he hadn't gotten around to fixing them yet. Then he said, "You wouldn't really hit a stiff, wouldja?"

Roger looked up. His eyes were laughing but his mouth stayed hard. "Why? It's not like they'd know it, would they?"

The old man rubbed his chin. "I suppose not."

"And what they don't know won't hurt them, right?"

The old man nodded slowly. "Nevertheless, it'd be bad luck."

It was Roger's turn to laugh. It was a rude laugh. "Speaking of luck, anyone around here ever score that receptionist?"

"Who? Carol? Hmm—" Old Jody shuffled toward the broom closet, shook his head. "Not that I know of."

"Just like I thought," said Roger. "Well, today's her lucky day."

***

Roger hung around for several hours beyond his shift. He washed his face in the men's room, then sat in the reception area reading an old copy of *Time*. Finally, at 7:55, Carol Shuftan walked in. To Roger's delight, she wore the same short tweed skirt she had on the first time he'd seen her. He was about to blurt out one of the three opening lines he'd been practicing when she upstaged him.

"What are *you* doing here?"

"Uh, I started looking at this magazine and just couldn't put it down." Roger held up the *Time*. "Ever read it?"

"Family resemblance?" she asked.

He looked at the cover of the magazine. It was a picture of a gorilla.

She strode by, forcing Roger to step aside lest she walk right over him. He tossed the magazine onto a chair and followed her into the hall. She was hanging her jacket in the closet. "Listen," he said to her back. "Maybe after work we could have a coffee or something?"

"I don't think so," she said, her back still turned.

"Then maybe a movie or—"

"Please." She turned sharply. "I get the message, okay? Thanks, but no thanks." Chilly. Twenty below.

Roger stood there blinking. "What'sa matter? You have a boyfriend?"

A smile crawled over her perfect mouth like a spider. "Not that it's any of your business, but no."

"Girlfriend?"

"Goodbye," she said, and she turned away.

He watched the object of six weeks worth of fantasies walk down the hall. Her ass wiggled beautifully as she walked. He decided that he was falling in love.

***

Roger spent the weekend with his brother Al drinking beer. Between the two, they knocked off two cases of Coors. Once Roger heard that Adolph Coors was an anti-Semite, that's all he would drink.

When he reported back to work Sunday evening, he noticed Bruce Young's Lexus parked in its reserved spot. Roger checked his watch. Quarter to ten. He was glad he was early. He made a point of passing the director's office and found Mr. Young sitting behind a huge cedar desk, engrossed in paperwork.

He stuck his head in the door.

"Hey, Mr. Young."

The older man looked up. "Oh, good evening, Roger."

"So how's about those Yankees?"

"Hmm? Oh, I didn't see the game last night. I've been very busy here, as you can imagine. Mark Shuftan was a dear friend of mine."

"Mark who?"

"Mark Shuftan. Carol's father—Oh, my! You've been away, haven't you? You didn't hear the news."

"What news?"

Bruce Young lowered his pen and stood up. He was tall, though slightly hunched over from age, a distinguished looking man with a sympathetic face. He bore a strong resemblance to his ancestor Jeremiah. "I regret having to tell you this, young man," he said, "but I'm afraid Carol was in an accident. Her car slid out of control Friday evening."

"Jeez," said Roger. "She okay?"

Mr. Young put his hand on Roger's shoulder. "No, son. I'm afraid not. Poor girl wasn't wearing her safety belt, apparently. She went right through the windshield."

"Wow," said Roger.

"A terrible tragedy," said Mr. Young. "Such a beautiful girl, and so sweet. Cut down in her prime. Bernie spent the entire day working on her. I supervised this one myself. She'll be beautiful for the wake tomorrow."

Roger was stunned as he left Bruce Young's office. He had a sick feeling in the pit of his gut. He walked toward the coffee machine and passed Jeremiah's picture. "What a waste," he said, looking up. "Tragic, huh Jerry? I mean, I wanted to fuck that bitch in the worst way."

***

It was 3 a.m. when Roger opened the door to the vault. The entire funeral home was cool, but this room was kept at 40 degrees Fahrenheit. That kept the bodies from smelling.

He noticed only one cadaver on a slab. It was under a sheet.

It's got to be her, he thought.

Roger walked over to the body. He could make out the figure of a woman beneath the sheet. At first Roger hesitated. He wanted to peek, but didn't care to see her all mangled and torn up. Then he remembered what Mr. Young had said about Bernie working on her all day.

He held the edge of the sheet and slowly inched it down.

In the dim light of the vault, he could see the top of her red hair sticking out from beneath the sheet. He pulled it down further and was grateful to discover that her eyes were closed. So he uncovered the rest of her face.

She was still startling, still such a beautiful face, though the life had clearly disappeared. The mortician had already applied lipstick, mascara, a touch of rouge.

Slowly, Roger drew back more of the sheet. That's when he saw the stitches. The accident had nearly decapitated her, but they'd done a nice job. Good old Bernie—by the time he dressed her tomorrow morning, buttoned to the top, no one would even notice. All they'd see was that lovely young face.

Through the sheet, Roger studied her naked breasts. They were as compelling as ever—large, firm. Her cruel nipples poked through the sheet.

Roger pulled the rest of the sheet back, right down to her waist. He stared at her.

"Pretty big tits," he said. "But hey, that don't make you a bad person." He extended his hand, brushed her nipple with his thumb. "Nice," he said.

Then he thought about it. *Really* thought about it.

And then he stopped thinking.

"What the fuck," he said out loud. "What they don't know won't hurt them."

And then he was on her.

***

At 5:58 a.m., Old Jody walked in and locked the big oak door behind himself.

"Mornin', Rog," he said.

"Hey, Jody."

"How'd it go last night?"

"You wouldn't believe me if I told you."

"One of the stiffs fart at you again?"

"Not exactly." Roger got up, threw on his jacket, and headed for the door. He was in a hurry to leave for a change, felt like he had a new lease on life. He smiled from ear to ear like a cat who'd swallowed a pigeon. Old Jody noticed, but didn't say anything.

Roger headed out the back door and broke into a slow jog, forgetting all about the steps that Old Jody was repairing. Suddenly, one step gave way and he went over backwards, slamming his head on a rock, and was knocked unconscious.

No one came near the back entrance until 9:37, when Rich Grunes, an O-ring salesman who'd come to pay his respects to Greg Shuftan's daughter, stepped out back for a cigarette. The doctor had been telling him to quit for a long time.

***

Roger's memory was vague, which is typical when you get hit on the head hard enough. The next thing he knew, there was a guy in a white lab coat standing over him. He recognized the man. It was Bernie, the mortician. He had a needle in his hand and he proceeded to inject something into Roger's arm.

Roger tried to sit up, but it was no use. He tried to speak, but couldn't do that either. He felt the needle go in deep, and something that felt like liquid fire shot through his veins. He wanted to scream. It hurt so badly, he wanted to cry. But all he could do was stare at Bernie. And then, suddenly, he couldn't see anything at all. Bernie had pulled the sheet over his face.

This is fucking unreal, Roger thought. They must think I'm dead. But if I'm dead—No, this is too crazy. I'll wake up soon. That's it. I'll just wake up—

Roger felt the sheet being pulled back again. This time, it was his Brother Al staring down at him.

"You're such as asshole, Rog," said Al. "Guess you won't be needing this." Roger felt Al slip his school ring off his finger. Then things went black again.

Sometime later, he felt the sheet come down once more. He looked up into the face of a strange man. The man was smiling. He was in his early twenties. He had blond hair and was clean shaven and wore a gold hoop in his right ear. Roger knew he had seen him somewhere before, but where?

Then he remembered.

It was the other guy who'd applied for his job; the one they'd hired as the alternate night watchman.

Roger felt the man touch his chest. What the fuck are you doing, he thought. But he couldn't say anything. Not a word.

He could feel everything all right, though—every bit of it, as the man roughly rolled him over on the slab and pulled off his underwear.

BRUISES

Living is easy with eyes closed
— John Lennon

The little boy's eyes twinkled big and brown and bright. His small mouth was wet and animated. His hair, disheveled, was healthy and long. And his cheeks wore a strong, rosy blush. In all, it was a beautiful face—a delightful face beaming with magic and wonderment, as most two-year-olds are wont to have. It was a pleasure to look at.

Except for the cuts. Except for those damn bruises.

Peter Jesinski assured the court that the lacerations were accidental; that they'd occurred when the child had fallen. There was no need for concern, he said. And the judge was forced to agree. That was the law. The Federal mandate for the preservation of families was quite clear. Despite Peter Jesinski's arrest record. Despite his history of drug abuse. Despite his problem with alcohol. Despite his recurrent violence in prison. Despite sanity and common sense and everything else that told the judge he was returning little Lance Jesinski to possible danger. The law was clear.

Pam Elder, the social worker assigned to the case, objected vehemently and red-eyed. There was firm evidence, she contested, that Lance was a victim of abuse. "Look at the pattern," she pleaded. "Look at the photographs!"

The judge held the photos at arm's length. His thumb print had already left smudges on each one. He shook his head slowly. "I'm sorry, Ms. Elder," he said, and he was. "The law is the law."

Peter Jesinski had passed two separate drug tests. He'd taken the six hours of mandatory parenting classes before Lance was removed from the state facility. The law said he was entitled to custody.

The law.

Is. The law.

"But the photographs," Pam pleaded. "The photographs are—"

"Subject to interpretation," said the judge. "Unless you provide this court with conclusive proof that this child is in danger, I have no choice but to return him to his father."

Peter Jesinski smiled like a lizard.

"Please, your honor—"

"That will be all, Ms. Elder. Motion denied."

"How's my boy?" Peter playfully clapped his son on the back of the head.

Lance smiled. He liked when his dad played with him. He liked riding in his dad's truck. He liked sunshine. He liked ice cream. "Can I have ice cream?" he asked.

"Why, sure," said his father.

Lance smiled. He played quietly with his tiny G.I. Joe as his dad drove the two home through the Sylmar area of the San Fernando Valley. He was glad to be going home and was lost in a fantasy world of war-play when they pulled into the driveway.

Michele was waiting at the door of the trailer. "Well?" she asked.

"Well what?" Peter replied.

"What did they say?"

"They said that boy sure better not show up with any more bruises."

"Jesus H. Christ, Peter! Didn't you tell them he fell down?"

"What do you *think* I told them?" Peter pushed his way passed the thin woman and dragged Lance into the four-room trailer home. He scratched his armpit, then headed for the kitchen. Inside the refrigerator, he pushed some things around. "There's no beer!" he announced.

"Then go get some, you lazy bastard," Michele yelled back from the other room.

Peter pulled his head out and slammed the refrigerator door. He headed back toward Michele. "Who you calling lazy?"

"Oh, knock it off."

"Didn't I warn you about that kind of talk, woman? This is my home, and you'd best remember it."

"Oh, will you shut the fuck up," she said. That cost her a slap in the mouth. Her lip smarted. She put her hand to it, winced, withdrew it and looked at the blood. "I guess someone's having a bad day," she said, her eyes no longer fixed on his.

Peter didn't answer. He flopped into an old easy chair—one of three pieces

BRUISES

of furniture in the room. He reached into his pocket and rooted around for his wallet, then checked his billfold, returned the stash to his trousers, and stood up again. "I'm getting beer," he said.

Michele raised the back of her hand to her still-throbbing lip. She watched him saunter out the front door again, then mumbled beneath her breath as he pulled out. She wanted to leave, too—and never return. But there was nowhere to go. At least the asshole pays the rent, she thought.

She headed toward the kitchen to get ice for her lip. That's where she found Lance. He was sitting in the middle of the floor, his hand deep in a container of ice cream. Chocolate trickled down his chin and lay in spotted puddles.

"What do you think you're doing?" she demanded.

The child looked up from his party and grinned.

"Look at this mess! You're a filthy pig! Clean yourself up this instant, you little bastard!"

Lance didn't understand filthy or pig or bastard. He did understand clean, though. He wanted to be clean, too. Clean felt nice. He wiped his sticky chocolate hands on his pants.

"Not on your damn clothes!" Michele reached down and grabbed him violently by the scruff of his shirt, hoisted him in the air and slapped his small face. Lance yelped.

"Don't you dare cry!" she demanded. "Just look what you did to my kitchen! Look at this mess!" She shook the screaming child. "I'm not your father! He spoils you rotten and you think you can get away with murder—but we'll just see about that."

Michele was still slapping Lance when the phone rang. She stopped to answer it.

"Hello? What? I can't hear you—SHUT UP!" she screamed at Lance. She covered her other ear. "Hello?"

"I said it's Susan. I'd have come over but I saw Peter's truck. Turn on channel nine, quick!"

"What's up?"

"Ricky Lake has these two black women on who don't know their husbands are cheatin' on them. It's hysterical!"

"Thanks," said Michele, searching for the remote. "I'll call you later."

By the time Peter returned with the beer, Ricky Lake was over. And Lance had cried himself to sleep.

***

"Your honor, this is the third time we've brought this man before you." Pam Elder stared at the judge with doe eyes. "Just look at these pictures."

The judge shook his head. Despite himself, he flipped through the photos for a third time. "These are inconclusive," he said.

"But clearly you can see a pattern established—"

"Not in my opinion," said the judge. "It's still circumstantial. You're asking me to separate a child from his parent. Do you have a witness?"

Pam didn't answer.

"No," said the judge. "You don't. And when you do, when you have the factors known as evidence, then I'll be eager to reopen this discussion. But until then, I must insist that you stop wasting this court's time with matters we can do nothing about."

"But your honor, if you would just—"

"Dismissed,' said the judge.

Pam left the courtroom with a knot in her stomach and a pounding in her temples. She wondered how things had reached this point; how society could place a criminal's rights before a victim's. She remembered that it hadn't always been this way. And she remembered a phone number.

Outside, she spotted Peter Jesinski descending the courthouse steps. She hesitated, bit her lip, then trotted over to him.

"Can I please speak with you?" she asked.

He halted and turned to her. "What about?"

"About your son. About what's best for Lance."

A slow smile crept over Peter's mouth. He snickered. "Little mousy woman like you's gonna tell me how to be a father, huh? That's a good one. That's real good."

"Look, Peter—cut the macho crap. I've spoken with you many times. I know you love your boy."

"Then why you trying to take him from me?"

"Because he's in danger, Peter!" Pam looked around, then lowered her voice. "He's in danger."

"From me? You really believe that?"

"Look at him," Pam said. "Look at his bruises. What do *you* think?"

"I never laid a hand on that boy in his entire life!" Peter's eyes were fierce and righteous "Swear to Christ!"

"Then how did he get that black eye?"

"Like I told the judge, he walked into a door."

"And the welt on his ear?"

"How the hell should I know? I work double shifts, goddamn it! Can't be there to watch every move he makes. If Michele says he walked into a door, then by Christ he walked into a door!"

"Michele?" asked Pam.

"My girlfriend," said Peter. "Watches the boy while I'm at work. But I'll tell you this—you keep hauling me into court and I'm gonna lose my job! Then I'm likely to get angry and somebody *will* get hurt!"

And with that, Peter Jesinski turned sharply and walked away.

***

Pam Elder paced her tiny bedroom. She couldn't sleep. She watered her hanging ferns, which didn't need watering; made certain her tropical fish were fed. Then she sat in her wing-back chair, gently stroking her Siamese cat, the line playing through her head, over and over, like an annoying jingle: Somebody *will* get hurt!

She looked at the clock by her bed table. 11:35 p.m., it said. Somebody *will* get hurt, it said. She stared at the phone. Somebody *will* get hurt!

She dialed the number that fear had committed to memory.

***

Outside the bedroom, Peter was fast asleep on the floor, a halo of crushed beer cans around his head. He was snoring. The television was screaming.

Inside the bedroom, the screaming was worse. Tears ran down the child's face. Michele was pinching him under his arm.

"I told you to shut up and go to sleep!" she yelled. "It's two o'clock in the morning! Now go to sleep!"

Lance gasped for breath. He was trying not to cry—but he was terrified. And Michele had pinched him again. Right on his boo-boo. Right where she'd pinched him yesterday. He tried to stop crying, but failed.

"SHUT UP!" Michele shook him. "You little bastard! You stupid—"

She stopped. She thought she heard the doorbell. It was hard to hear anything above the child's screaming. She put her hand over his mouth. Then she heard it again. Definitely the door. She put Lance down, shut the lights, and slammed the door behind her. He'd cry himself to sleep again, she decided, wondering who in hell would visit at this time of the morning.

She opened the door.

Something solid hit her in the face, knocking her over backward. She hit the floor with a heavy thud. Then she felt something go soft inside as a boot caught her in the stomach. Then again. And again... Doubled up, she

coughed blood, tried to call for Peter, but all she could do was fight for breath. She felt the boot once more—felt her ribs crack and move. She knew she was bleeding inside. She was nauseous. The pain was exquisite. But she had little time to savor it because the next blow crushed her skull.

***

Peter used a public defender. He had no money for an expensive attorney. Besides, why should he need one, he thought. He'd done nothing wrong. Someone had murdered his girlfriend. Someone had kidnapped his child while he slept.

The prosecutor didn't buy it. Neither did the jury. Or perhaps they all knew better but didn't care. After all, Peter Jesinski hadn't cared about his own child. Not enough. The pictures proved that much, if nothing else. And Pam Elder's testimony confirmed it. Peter Jesinski may have been innocent of *these* crimes, but he'd been guilty of *others*.

Pam Elder went home after the trial—home to her hanging ferns and her tropical fish and her Siamese cat; home to her herb garden and her collection of candy tins and her tiny one-bedroom apartment. It was getting small, she thought. She'd have to find a larger place, soon.

Especially now that the family was growing.

Deprogramming Esther

"Do you see any progress?"

Rabbi Brecht emerged from behind the heavy locked door. He ignored the question until he had latched the door again, this time from the outside. Then he turned to his old friend and smiled. It was a deliberate smile, meant to offer encouragement. "Be patient," Brecht replied. He placed a pudgy, hairy hand on the other rabbi's shoulder. "These things take time. Be confident that you've come to the right place."

Rabbi Kitzer tried to return the smile, but only half of his mouth responded. His eyes, wet and small behind thick, smudged glasses, betrayed the weight of his fear. This was the most difficult thing in the world for him, to see his child so broken, confused—so *farmischt*. But he *had* come to the right place. He knew that. Amongst Hassidim, Shlomo Brecht was considered the preeminent cult-buster, the best money could buy. If anybody could bring Kitzer's daughter back to her senses, it was Brecht.

Kitzer drew greedily on what was left of his cigarette, then the little man squashed the butt into an ashtray littered with filters. He sighed a heavily as he pulled at his beard. "You won't hurt her?" he asked. It wasn't a question. He was pleading.

Brecht shook his head with practiced bedside theatrics. "We won't hurt her," he promised.

Behind the locked door, the room air was stale and warm, like the inside of a high school locker room after a game. A gray despondency seemed to hang over everything. Shabby, long-outdated curtains were drawn on the windows, making it impossible to discern whether it was day or night. The only light source was a single bulb obscured by a cheap, brown paper shade. There was scarcely any furniture in the tiny room. A cot, unmade at present, had been haphazardly shoved into the corner opposite the window. The only other furnishings were an old wooden table in the center of the room, and two chairs that faced each other. Seated in one, a frail girl of perhaps nineteen chewed off what little polish was left on her thumbnail. She wore a bright yellow sundress that fell just above the knee. The frock appeared as if she'd slept in it for two days, which she had. There was nothing about her face particularly memorable—it was just pale, particularly in the cruel light cast by the single bulb. She wasn't a homely girl, but rather plain, and her eyes and mouth could have done with a touch of makeup, but she wore none. Her lips were chapped and drawn tight, a thin little gash; her deep-set eyes, wild, like those of a caged monkey.

"They'll come for me," she said for the tenth time in half as many hours. "You'll see. They'll come."

"Who'll come for you, Esther?" The young assistant rabbi seated opposite the girl rested his bearded face in his hands with his elbows planted firmly on the table.

"You know damn well who!"

"Oh, Esther," scolded the rabbi. "Rabbi Brecht and I keep telling you: No foul language." He smiled sweetly at the young girl.

"Go to hell," she said.

Outside the locked door, Kitzer paced. The sweat made his balding head glisten and itch, and he removed his *yarmulke* to scratch it with the skullcap. Nervously, he walked the floorboards muttering to himself, alternating between the Psalms of David that he'd memorized as a boy and scolding himself in a hybrid Yiddish-English.

"*Abishter!*" he said, entreating the Almighty. "What did I do? Help me understand where I went wrong. I sent my children to yeshiva!"

He had peeked in on his daughter earlier that morning. She'd ignored him—just sat in her dress—Ach! Sleeveless! Like a *shikse*, sleeveless!—her arms folded in defiance. "This is my daughter?" he had asked her, his voice rising. "This *oppikoras*?"

She wouldn't even look at him.

That's what she is, he now thought as he paced the room. An *oppikoras*. An apostate. One who denies scripture.

Kitzer's eyes grew watery again. He reached for another cigarette but found the pack was finished, so he went back to pacing and reciting.

Behind the locked door, out of earshot from anyone on the other side, Rabbi Brecht was doing his job. "You should be ashamed of yourself!" he shrieked. "*Ashamed!*" It had been two days. Two days of questioning the girl as to her whereabouts, her associates, her reasons for leaving the forty-year-old Lubavitcher Community that had been founded by her own grandfather.

Brecht and his assistants wanted to know everything.

Esther told them nothing, just sat there vacillating between anxiety and loathing, picking at her nails, smoothing her dress, flatly refusing to cooperate. She watched Brecht pull back slightly. For the last hour he had been only inches away, his garlic-and-coffee breath hot in her face. It sickened her, the screaming, that breath, the omnipresent awareness of being trapped and not knowing how or when she would escape. *If* she would escape.

Two days. Two full days. She wanted to scream. She wanted to vomit.

"Your poor father!" Brecht yelled. "Your poor mother!"

"Don't talk about my mother!" Esther screeched.

Brecht stopped. He had hit a chord. Good, good! He watched a tear run down the girl's cheek and land upon the wooden table.

"You don't know *anything* about my mother!"

"I know that she is a good Jewish woman who loves her children very much."

"*Love?*" said Esther, the word dripping with sarcasm. "She's never shown me love. She's never shown any of us love—not my brothers, not my father. She doesn't know the meaning of the word. She makes me sick. *You* make me sick."

"How can you say this?" the rabbi exploded, matching her righteous indignation with his own. He knew he was breaking through. "For a child to say a mother doesn't love? Doesn't care for her husband? It's a *shondah*. How can be such a thing? *You* know so much about love? *You're* the expert on love? Of *course* your mother loves your father. How were you born, *nu*?"

Esther pulled back. In an instant, the entire context of her situation had shifted. She ceased looking at Brecht as something loathsome and contemptible. Now she viewed him as stupid.

"You think that's love, rabbi?" She spoke the word *rabbi* like a gang-banger says asshole. *Exactly* the way a gang-banger says asshole. "That's not love," she said. "That's sex. That's people having intercourse. That's fucking. Like animals."

Outside the room, Kitzer awoke in the chair he'd passed out in. His back hurt; his neck was stiff. Brecht had urged him to go home—to be with his wife and other children. Trust the professionals to do their jobs.

"We've saved so many children," Brecht assured him. "Hundreds. Maybe more—I can't keep track. They get them and fill them with dangerous ideas. You can't imagine. I know because I deal with it, but you shouldn't know from it. What with the drugs and the atheism—you shouldn't know. So they come to me, the parents, and I work with their children. We get to the root

of their problems, break them of their need for a cult. We find new solutions. Your daughter will come back to you. You'll see."

But Kitzer hadn't gone home. He couldn't leave his daughter alone. Not now.

Not that he was so anxious to get back home, either. Once there, his wife would scream; she'd scold and criticize him, belittle and blame him. Chaya had to blame someone, Kitzer thought. He tried to be understanding. But he was in no hurry to get back home.

The small man pulled at his beard, then reached into his breast pocket. When he withdrew it, he held a crumpled sheet of paper. A letter. He thought to read it again, but just stared at it until his blood boiled and his breath grew short. Then he returned the letter to his pocket.

* * *

Inside the dark room, Esther was crying. It had been three days, and today had been the worst. Today they had shown her the movies.

At first, she refused to watch. She wasn't a fool—she knew the films were designed to agitate her and wear her down. But the compelling nature of the scenes they played made it difficult *not* to watch.

The first movies were of children—little Jewish children. Playing. Laughing. Learning Torah. Esther smiled for the first time in three days. She loved children. More than anything. It was an instinct augmented by the experience of raising her younger brothers. The teenage girl had been expected to feed and clothe and diaper and coddle every family member younger than she was, meaning all of them.

Without warning, Brecht switched films. Now Esther watched in horror as the brownshirts goose-stepped along the streets of Berlin. She watched as thousands and tens of thousands Seig-Heiled their Führer, the angel of death; watched as Jews lined the street en masse for deportation to the labor camps; watched as her people were paraded naked, men and women and their children before them, loaded onto cattle cars, then herded through forests toward open pits where they were gunned down like animals; watched as charred bodies were removed from ovens for burial or, worse, left half-alive because the efficiency of the killing machine had somehow slipped a cog.

And as she watched, she listened—listened to the meaty voice of Rabbi Brecht; listened as he read aloud accounts from Auschwitz, Treblinka, Majdanek, Bergen-Belsen; listened to the cold statistics, to the tales of Jewish babies tossed in the air for sport and caught on the bayonets of German soldiers; listened to the stories of men who'd watched as their wives' breasts were hacked off and thrown to German shepherds; listened to details of painful experimentations by German physicians on their Jewish patients, to endless survivors' accounts of torture and rape and truncheons and...

"Enough!" Esther screamed.

Brecht stopped reading.

"Enough! Enough!" the girl cried.

"This is our punishment!" said Brecht.

"I can't hear this anymore!"

"This is what the Almighty sends upon His nation. This is the blessing and the curse. If we keep His commandments, then we shall prosper, we and our children; we shall live in the land of milk and honey with our righteous *Moshiach*. But if we turn away, Heaven forbid, if we turn away from His good teachings, then this is what happens, Esther! In every generation, Esther! To *all* Jews, Esther!"

"Please!" she cried, the tears pouring from her reddened eyes. "Please! I want to see my father!"

Outside the room, Kitzer recited the *brucha* over bread, then pulled a stale piece of crust from his sandwich and nibbled at it. He wasn't really hungry. What little appetite he'd achieved was squelched by his wife who had screamed at him on the phone for the last ten minutes.

"I want you home, *now!*"

"Chaya, you're not being reasonable. Esther is our daughter. This is a frightening time for her. She needs to know that her father is here. It's just a few more..."

"This house is a wreck and the children are running around like wild Indians, and if you hadn't been so liberal with that girl in the first place..."

Kitzer took another nibble, then flipped the sandwich into a trash can in the corner of the room. He pulled the letter out of his pocket for the fifth time. This time he unfolded it and read.

Dear Rabbi Kitzer:

College can be a difficult time for any student. This is especially true for those from troubled homes, or when parents object to their children leaving the nest. Despite the thirst for knowledge, overcoming the guilt of displeasing parents makes adjusting to a new environment even more strenuous than it might otherwise be.

As Dean of Students, part of my job is smoothing the transition period for co-eds. Consequently, I asked Esther to advise me of her progress here, and to keep me abreast of developments at home. Assuming her reports to be truthful, I am saddened by what I hear: That her communication with her parents has been abated, with lectures and harsh words serving as poor substitutes. Despite your initial disapproval when Esther enrolled, I h ad hoped you were interested in maintaining a dialogue with her. Clearly, that has not been the case.

I am further saddened to hear that you blame Esther for the problems in your home. I am writing because, having met you, I discern that you are intelligent and sensitive enough to know that this cannot be the case. That we are only victims of our own choices, and that Esther's relationship with you and your wife is a by-product of her upbringing, not the education she receives at Saint Lawrence. To suggest to Esther that her attending a university is "shortening the life of her father" is, in my opinion, both manipulative and singularly lacking in compassion. The guilt in which you attempt to envelop her may have ramifications far into her future. Asserting that her desire for secular education is "a serious problem... a result of sickness," as you recently wrote her, is, in a word, preposterous.

I have closely observed Esther this semester. I have studied her psychological profile and spent long hours discussing her goals. We have also delved into the obstacles she encounters as an Orthodox Jew studying outside the confines of the community she grew up in.

What I have concluded is this: Esther is a remarkable young woman. She is intelligent, brave, and extraordinarily self-aware. The problem is not Esther. It is the hostility she faces at home.

When we last spoke, you expressed your fear that Esther would abandon the customs she was raised to respect. At that time, I advised you to help her find room for education within the confines of your traditions; to enable her growth, and not attempt to stunt it. This would only force her away from you, which is the precise opposite of what you seek. Nevertheless, your wife's steadfastness on the subject has gone far beyond the parameters of normal behavior. It is difficult for me to even imagine a mother championing a petition against her own daughter, an action that served to isolate Esther from your community.

Esther is convinced that your participation in family matters would go a long way toward eliminating these hostilities. Nevertheless, she says you spend little time at home. That instead you prefer "Hassidic Farbrengens," the frequent gatherings in your community where men drink and sing songs.

I must admit, sir, that I am at a loss when it comes to the specific customs of your community. Although I have the greatest respect for your traditions, and I am myself Jewish, I question an environment that discourages affection between family members, as Esther reports is the case in your home. I know many Orthodox Jews who report that there are no such stringencies in their doctrine. Consequently, I wonder whether this is indeed part of your culture, or merely another family anomaly.

In my professional opinion, Esther is relatively healthy, despite these obstacles. And she is on the road to even greater health. She is making friends here, excelling in her studies, and far happier now than when she first arrived. Moreover, I assure you that she has not abandoned belief in her religion, but only some of the rigors of Eighteenth Century European culture. Given half a chance, I am certain that you will be proud of the woman she is developing into.

Please call me day or night if I can be of further assistance.

Sincerely yours,

Paul M. Freedlander, Dean of Students

Kitzer folded the letter once again and placed it in his breast pocket. He wanted a cigarette. Suddenly, the latch of the door was thrown. He looked up as Rabbi Brecht emerged.

"Your daughter," said Brecht, "would like to see you."

***

Neither father nor daughter spoke on the trip home. Esther slept through most of the three-hour journey. Kitzer stopped only once on the road, at a gas station to inspect the air in his tires and to ask the attendant to check his oil. Both were fine. As the attendant closed the hood, Kitzer looked over at Esther and said a silent prayer of thanks. She had agreed not to return to Saint Lawrence. She had promised, instead, to attend the Lubavitcher Seminary in Montreal. Kitzer was grateful to have her back.

Gently, so not to wake her, Kitzer leaned over and popped open his glove compartment, then reached inside and produced a notebook. Brecht had confiscated the book from Esther. On the cover were the words "Creative Writing 101: Esther Kitzer."

Kitzer opened it and began to read an essay entitled "Cripples."

Who could know what it's like to watch your family grow into nothingness? My brothers are kept from learning English. They're forbidden to read non-Hassidic books. They're talented, they're smart, but they're made into cripples, people without education, people with no proper way of expressing themselves creatively or emotionally. My mother seems to take pleasure in stifling their creativity. She squashes their inquisitiveness, slaps at their childishness, and rages at their burning need to love each other, a love she has grown violently jealous of and does not believe in.

My parents are so concerned with their own concepts of Good versus Evil that they fear anything different or new. They fail to understand a person's need for choice. And that when you remove that freedom, people are no longer good or bad—they're just robots.

My father arrives on the scene only to entertain or give advice like some enlightened Solomon to an adult daughter who has grown beyond the need for his counsel. How could he send his adolescent daughter off to boarding school for five years and then expect, out of nowhere, to suddenly emerge as my father? He doesn't even know me. He made no effort in all those years to communicate with me or discover who I was and what I was growing into.

Kitzer closed the notebook. He looked upon his daughter's fragile face, pale in the bright summer sunshine. He wanted to say something, maybe ask if she'd like to stop for a soda. Yes, that was a good idea—all kids liked soda.

He opened his mouth to speak, but ended up clearing his throat. Decided to let her sleep instead. Kids need their sleep, he thought. He didn't look at her again for the entire journey.

***

It was three days later. Kitzer sat in his office. He had just hung up with his brother in Montreal and was settling down to learn from his *Tanya* when the phone rang. He hoped it was his brother calling back with good news—news that Esther's lodgings had been secured in a real *Chassidishe* home. He picked up the phone with confidence and relief.

It was not his brother. It was the police.

Esther had been rushed to the hospital. Two of her little brothers had found her at home, passed out, an empty bottle of sleeping pills by her side.

Kitzer jumped from his chair, knocking the *Tanya* to the floor. He rushed from the building, jumped into his station wagon, and drove toward the hospital.

"Please let her be all right," he prayed. "Please, please..."

God answered Kitzer's prayers.

God said no.

***

The funeral was held the next day. That is the Jewish way. Esther had died after sundown. Another sun could not be allowed to set before she was laid to rest.

The entire community attended the funeral. Kitzer didn't notice them. All he could see was the plain pine box being carried down the hill to the six-foot ditch. He recited the *kaddish*, then turned to leave.

"Rabbi Kitzer?"

The voice came from behind him. Kitzer turned back.

"I'm sorry, Rabbi Kitzer," said the man. "Terribly sorry. She was a fine girl." It was Paul M Freedlander, Dean of Students of Saint Lawrence University.

"Yes," said Kitzer. "She was very special. Thank you for coming." Kitzer met Freedlander's eyes as he shook the man's extended hand. He knew it was customary for mourners to specifically not shake hands, but at the moment he didn't much care for specifics.

As the procession left, Kitzer spotted his wife and younger children. His three-year-old had found a worm and was playing with it. His wife slapped the child across the face. "You don't play with *sh'rotzim* at a funeral!" she screamed.

Kitzer put his hands in his pockets. He found a stray cigarette there and brought it to his lips, but didn't light it. Then he removed it again, crushed it, and let it fall to the ground.

He decided to return home alone. As he walked, he wondered what he'd look like without a beard.

For "Rebbetzin" Chaya Teitelbaum:
Ask not for whom the spigots rust.

A Day in The Death of Martin Peel

Don't surround yourself with yourself.
— Jon Anderson

Martin Peel pressed the Browning to his forehead and pulled the trigger, sending the nine-millimeter Parabellum projectile through his right temple at twelve-hundred and twenty-five feet-per-second, punching a hole where it entered approximately the size of a dime and, where it exited, roughly that of a handball. He didn't experience the creation of these apertures; didn't feel his bladder release and the warm trail of acrid-smelling urine stream down the inside of his pants leg. He didn't have to clean the expensive Persian rug of flesh chunks and bloody pulp that were once the gray matter of his brain, a brain that had turned self destructive from bad programming and bad chemicals; the mess, as always, was left for others. He experienced no sensations at all as the essence of what was Martin Peel sailed out of the meat shell he had always thought of as Martin Peel.

He had planned it correctly. A quick death. A swift escape. Better than he deserved, most people would agree. It was only when Martin found himself in the theater that he realized his plan had been thwarted.

Martin Peel left behind a thirty-year-old wife named Jennifer, who everyone called Jin, and two little girls named Rae and Kelly, ages seven and five. Martin was thirty-five when his finger squeezed the trigger of the High-Power semi-automatic, the gun he'd paid nearly four-hundred dollars for and kept in his sock drawer throughout his nine-year marriage. He'd lied to Jin when he bought the weapon. Said he wanted to protect their home. But the truth was Martin and Jin's home needed little protection, being fully alarmed and situated in a white residential neighborhood called Cedar Woods where the only crime ever committed was tax evasion. One reason Martin bought the gun was because he suspected he might one day do himself in. It was a sus-

picion he never voiced. The other reason for the gun was paranoia—a recurrent anticipation of defending his home against militant Jew haters, as his grandparents had failed to do when their next-door neighbor turned them over to the S.S. during Krakow's "house cleaning" of 1939. Martin's father and his Uncle Nate were sent to forced labor at Plaszów and survived, more or less. His grandparents and their other five children were shipped to

Auschwitz and did not survive by any stretch of the imagination, *yahrzeit* candles and plaques on the shul's eternal memorial wall notwithstanding. Two decades after the war ended, Uncle Nate boarded a 727 out of Kennedy Airport to Brussels, then rented a car and drove all the way to Krakow where he found his ex-neighbor residing in his parents' old home. There, Uncle Nate stuck a six-inch blade into his ex-neighbor's stomach and, with what he later described as a certain relish, tore out his ex-neighbor's ex-entrails and was back in Flatbush eating boiled cabbage before the Krakow *policja* even discovered the body.

Growing up, Martin had tremendous affection for Uncle Nate. The old man gave him Buffalo Head nickels whenever the family visited, and a copy of Meir Kahane's *Never Again* for his bar-mitzvah. Uncle Nate had massive forearms from working as a baker and carrying forty-pound sacks of flour up the steps of his basement. Three years before Martin blew holes in his head, Uncle Nate came down with cancer of the colon, and then cancer of the everything.

The newspapers said Martin Peel was thirty-four when he died. The newspapers were off by a year. No one knows how the papers made that mistake, nor whose fault it was. Not that it mattered.

Martin was not alone in the theater. There were many people with him, and he recognized most of them. Some were relatives. He looked around, studied their faces. Uncle Nate wasn't there. As he stared, Martin realized that there was no one present he liked very much. While he was alive, these were people he snickered about, told Jin he hated, though it wasn't true. Martin hated fewer people than he claimed to. The thought came to him like an epiphany.

He looked around some more, then had another revelation: The people in the room didn't hate him either. They pitied him.

It was a horrible discovery.

The newspapers did not say why Martin Peel killed himself. They didn't know the reason, and wouldn't have printed it if they had.

The reason Martin committed suicide was because he thought he was punishing himself. He believed the most loathsome thing on the whole bastard planet was a bully.

He himself had been the victim of bullies as a child. The first bully to torment him was Johnny Rubin, the son of a urologist who lived across the street from Martin's family in Rockaway, New Jersey. Martin was five years old when Johnny, who was nine, and his younger sister Jamie, who was six-and-a-half, moved in. Martin had stood near the rose bushes at the corner of his property watching two sweaty negroes unload the Allied Van Lines truck when he first saw Jamie and Johnny dart out from their expensive new split-level. Johnny was chasing his sister with a bathrobe tie-cord, snapping it at her, attempting to give her what kids called a rat-tail. The horsing around made Martin excited. In an effort to join in, he picked up a rock and hurled it at the two chasing children. A lucky shot landed the stone in Jamie's eye.

Jamie didn't lose her eye, nor did she have any permanent damage to her eyesight, but she wore a patch for several days. She grew up to forget all about the incident and develop into an attractive, popular teenager. By age sixteen, she became active in her high school drama club and was considered a promising talent by teachers until she began smoking marijuana and hanging out with a bad crowd. By the time she graduated, Jamie was no longer interested in thespian activities, and her grade point average had slipped to a C-. At her graduating class's tenth year reunion, the only thing classmates still remembered about Jamie Rubin was that she had blown six guys on the football team in the locker room one afternoon.

It wasn't even true, but people remembered it anyway.

As for Johnny Rubin, he tortured young Martin from the day his sister was tagged by that rock. He organized the other kids on the block, convinced them to shun Martin, forbidding the little boy's participation in kickball or hopscotch or any of a dozen other pastimes on Wenonah Avenue. One day, on the way home from school, all the kids lined up to punch Martin in the stomach.

Evoking profound relief in both Martin and his parents, whose only advice to that point had been stay away from the Rubin boy, Johnny Rubin graduated high school and went off to college when Martin was still in eighth grade.

Four years later, when Martin was seventeen, his mother surprised him with a blast from the past. "You'll never guess who I ran into," she said as she walked into the kitchen carrying a bag of fresh-smelling baked goods.

"Huh?"

"I saw Johnny Rubin at the Viking Bakery. He works there part-time. He's become a very nice young man."

Later that evening, Martin and two of his friends drove out to Mountain Lakes, New Jersey, where Johnny and his sister Jamie and their urologist father and their professionless mother had moved three years earlier. Everybody thought Mountain Lakes was controlled by the Mafia. It was certainly a safe neighborhood. Martin and his friends waited in the parking lot across from the Viking. They sat in their car and watched as the lights turned off inside the bakery. Then Johnny Rubin emerged and locked the front door.

"My Uncle Nate used to own a bakery," said Martin offhandedly as he watched the scene. The three teenagers sat motionless as Johnny Rubin crossed the street and headed toward them.

"That's the one?" asked one of Martin's friends, a teenager of Polish descent named Dave who would join the Marines six months after this incident.

"Yup," said Martin.

The three teens exited the car, a '72 Mercury Montego whose engine would seize four months after this incident. They hastened their pace toward Johnny Rubin, who was just a few car lengths away fishing for his keys in the deep pocket of the white pants he wore when working at the bakery. Martin was the first to reach him. He hit Rubin with a billyclub across the shoulder, then again on the back. Then he kicked Rubin in the ribs while his two friends kicked Rubin in different places.

The entire episode lasted about a minute until the older boy was semi-conscious, with several broken ribs and his lip torn partly off, exposing broken bloodied teeth. Then the three boys left Rubin wet and moaning and went out for beers. The beers were on Martin. No one could say he wasn't a stand-up guy.

Martin could not see the walls of the theater. Neither could he see any other details, the seats, a projector, or even a screen, though he assumed each element was in place. The only things he could see were the faces all around him—some he had known all his life. He assumed these people had come to witness against him, or to act as a jury. The reason Martin thought this was because he was conscious of being the center of attention, which made him feel as if he was on trial.

He wasn't, of course. The trial was long since over.

Jin cried at Martin's funeral. The only other person who cried was Dave, Martin's friend who had once joined the Marines. Dave was a vacuum cleaner salesman for Electrolux, now. He managed his own franchise.

As they lowered Martin's casket into the ground, Jin clutched her two little girls tightly by their hands. She remembered how in love she had been with Martin when they were first married. She thought he was the most clever and intense man she had ever met.

Intense. That was the word she used to describe him to her friends. Martin was intense. The way he spoke; the way he took over a situation. The way he made love to her. The first time Martin blackened her eye, that was intense, too. Only Jin didn't use that word to describe it.

She was thinking about the black eye when they covered Martin's coffin with dirt.

Martin watched the images dance in front of him. Everything was familiar—incidents Martin had lived, scenes he had seen through his own eyes as he lived them. Somehow, the emotions Martin felt when he first experienced those moments were resurrected, too. This was a more accurate playback device than the machine Martin had once called his memory. He was very curious about it, this device, but his curiosity was only momentary—the emotions that flooded over him were too intense to be denied.

Intense.

Martin saw a little girl's eye peering through the peephole in the concrete tunnel. It was the summer of 1967, which Hippies in Haight-Ashbury were calling the Summer of Love. Martin was six years old. His mother had brought him to Fireman's Field, a lovely green park she was fond of, and set him loose to play among the other children in the fenced-in square as she read about Jeannie Shrimpton in the latest issue of *Redbook*.

Martin scurried into an oblong, concrete tunnel that was just high enough for small children to stand in and larger children to crawl through. There were lots of other boys and girls of various ages playing nicely in the tunnel, racing around it, peering through the peep holes.

He spied a little girl, a delicate blonde about his own age wearing a thin purple flowered dress. He asked her if she wanted to play. Then Martin led his new playmate around the outside of the tunnel and told her to remain there as he scampered back inside and grabbed a handful of dusty sand. He waited. A moment later, her little eye, as blue as a robin's egg, pressed up against the opening. Martin tossed the fine white sand—

A jolt ripped through Martin and he screamed. He was still in the theater, still watching the images before him, but his entire body was racked with pain and revulsion, with regret and humiliation, with fear and horror and the burning, scalding sensation of fine white sand in a naked eye. Martin fought to wipe the sand away and was eventually successful. Then he opened his eyes again. Just in time to see the next image.

Rae and Kelly were sent to a therapist. The therapist gave them grape lollipops and tried to get them to talk about their father. The therapist wanted the girls to say they missed him. She told Jin it was best for the children not to suppress their feelings.

Rae, who was seven, had this to say: "I don't really miss him so much. He yelled a lot. Sometimes he bought me toys and I liked the toys."

Kelly, who was five, wanted to know if being dead hurt.

"I can't take it anymore!" Martin screamed as tears streamed down his cheeks. "Please!" he cried overwhelmed by nausea. "Have some fucking pity! Don't they have any fucking pity?"

They, apparently, had no fucking pity whatsoever. *They*, whoever, they were, continued to show Martin Peel the scenes of his life.

He was shown the time he slammed his mother in the ear with Dr. Seuss's *Green Eggs And Ham* when he was still in second grade—a stunt that, curiously, received no punishment. Then he watched himself steal a little boy's hockey cards when he was ten. Then he was shown the unpopular, obese girl in high school that he and his friends called Lump. Then he was shown the evening he got drunk and broke his father's arm in four places with a wine bottle. Then he was shown the scores of girls he'd pretended to care about until he had gotten in their pants, including the one he'd impregnated. Then, he was shown the aborted fetus.

"Please!" Martin screamed. "*Please!*" His throat was raw. His stomach was lava. The scenes played on for hours into days, endlessly, the pain they invoked building, one upon another, each one more painful than the last. Now he was watching Jin looking into his eyes and crying. She was asking, "How could you do this to me? It's bad enough you hit me, but another woman? Oh God, Martin. Oh God—"

—And that's when the images stopped. As suddenly as they had begun.

The screen in front of Martin was black. As black as coal. As black as the blackest black hole.

Martin trembled involuntarily. It was as if every nerve ending in his body had been ignited; every emotion wrung dry. His breathing was shallow; his head pounded. He was all at once drained and exhausted and sick and terrified.

He blinked his eyes. And when he opened them again, there was a new image in front of him. A very different image.

It was Martin Peel. A happy Martin Peel. A content Martin Peel.

He watched himself playing patiently with his daughters in the park... walking hand in hand with Jin through a moonlit evening... receiving warm greetings from co-workers... experiencing genuine fellowship at parties... fishing with his father... attending ball games with his brother-in-law... volunteering time at the orphanage... being honored by his peers...

Martin watched dozens of such scenes—watched a Martin Peel he didn't know experiencing moments he couldn't recall.

"I don't understand," he heard himself say. "Why can't I remember these things?"

No one answered him. *They*, whoever they were, knew he'd figure it out soon enough. That he'd realize he was not watching the Martin Peel who *was*, but the Martin Peel who *could have been*. That this, above all else, was the most just punishment that could be doled out to a man: To see oneself as one might have been. If only.

If only.

"No, Kelly," said the therapist. "No sweetheart. Being dead doesn't hurt."

Of course, the therapist wasn't telling the truth to little Kelly. But she wasn't aware of it at the time, and it's not really a lie if you're not aware of the truth.

And even if it *is* a lie, there's much worse things.

Much worse things, Martin.

PART TWO

THE SAGA OF HANK MAGITZ

DREW'S GIRLFRIEND

It's possible I'd been listening to Morrison too much that week, or perhaps it was the beer. or the tequila. either way, it was obvious from the moment I walked into the bar that I was hungry, brewing, radiating trouble, a heat seeker. Mike saw it. Round Rich saw it. Jim's tramp Terry saw it, too, but didn't recognize it—women can't read trouble like men can. obviously.

so I'm through the door and the first thing I do is scan for bad asses. I spot these two skinhead fucks in the corner to my left, just outside the ladies' room. I mark that. the rest of the place was soft, soft as slime, so I throttled down and checked out the women. the best was a brunette (naturally) in a purple satin blouse, sitting at the opposite corner of the bar. there was an arm draped gingerly around her. belonged to a geek.

I was still staring at her when Jim's tramp, who had been up front watching Jim sing, came over. she asked if this was the first time I'd seen Jim's band play and I said yeah, after five years, what the fuck. They were pretty good, too. Jim had a wonderful robust voice, very macho, and he was performing the latest radio spew—Stone Temple Pilots, Bush, Smashing Pumpkins, but then he'd castrate it between songs, chatting up the audience, real cornball and squeaky, so the mystique was shot all to hell. but the guy at the bar with the brunette was digging it, yukking it up. killed me. what a waste of good woman. I watched her stand up and head toward the ladies' room. it was her second trip in fifteen minutes.

Jim's tramp headed back toward the band as I ordered another beer. the geek saw her and dropped his arm around her. real friendly geek. after a bit, I decided he'd kept it there too long.

I leaned over and whispered to Jim's friend Loren, "who's the guy with his arm around Jim's tramp?"

"just Drew. he's a dork."

"how'd a dork end up with that brunette at the bar?"

"in his *dreams*," she said. "he's just hoping."

"mmm," I said.

I watched the band a bit, until Mike came over and bought me another beer. then Round Rich came over and asked how drunk I was.

"what kind of asshole question is that?" he hadn't learned any manners in San Francisco. of course, he hadn't gone there to learn manners. went there to chase this crazy bitch he'd been after since high school—the one who blew my buddy Dave in the parking lot at Friendly's while her boyfriend was spooning down a vanilla Fribble.

"ask me what my shirt says?"

Rich looked at the sweatshirt, big Japanese characters on a rising sun.

"what's it say?"

"what's what say?"

"your shirt."

"I'd tell you," I said, stepping into his face, "but then I'd have to kill you." which answered both questions.

"so kill me."

"shut up," I said. "I'm practicing."

"buy you a beer?"

"black and tan," I said, and Rich repeated it to the bartender as the brunette made her way back from the ladies' room. I caught her eye. she smiled.

"'scuse me,' I said, getting up and moving toward her.

"don't do it " said Rich. "that's Drew's girlfriend."

"don't know Drew," I said.

"he's my friend."

"every dickless loser that walks into this bar is your friend." I lifted my beer and made my way toward the brunette.

her name was Chris. with a C, she said. so I kept calling her that. she looked even better up close. really nice eyes and eyebrows. my type. and she liked me, too—liked me way better than Drew did.

"you're one of Jim's friends?" she asked.

"yup."

"musician?"

"writer."

"really? what do you write?"

"hard to say. it's never the same."

she smiled. great smile. great teeth. little white soldiers all in a row. "what's your shirt say?"

ten minutes later, she excused herself and headed toward the ladies' room again. I watched her walk away. then I inched over to Drew.

"your girlfriend goes the bathroom a lot," I said. he didn't answer. maybe it was the shirt. "that's the third time in twenty minutes. if she was with me, she'd hold it in."

Rich tapped me on the shoulder. "get me high," he said.

"I'm working."

"this is wrong," he yelled in my ear, over the band—they were really loud and we were right up front. "you shouldn't hit on Drew's girlfriend."

"she isn't his girlfriend," I said. "he doesn't stand a chance."

"not with you moving in."

I looked over at Drew. geek. dork. washed out. loser. like everyone else in the bar and on the street and outside and me, let's face it. only he wasn't doing anything about it. which makes all the difference.

besides, I was just screwing around. until I got a few shots of tequila into her and into me. and then the sonic thoughts hit like Vesuvias, and you forget all about having to drive home on slippery roads, and having somewhere to be the next morning, and having a wife and kids and what that means.

only for a second. which is long enough.

"okay," I said, but Round Rich didn't hear it because the music was too loud and nobody could hear a goddamn thing, and I was already somewhere on the other side of the room, head throbbing, looking for a skinhead to bludgeon.

Another Joe Story

Joe was hurt, and I guess he had a right to be—no one sees themselves as others see them, and rarely as I portray them in a story. More heroic, perhaps. At least smarter. Joe felt I had only captured some basic part of him and left out something essential. He confronted me with this at the party.

"Do you still care about me?" Really loaded the dice with that one, but it was only our friends and a few wives and kids. No need to play it macho.

"Course I care," I said. "What did I do now?" Figured it was the way I'd snarled at him that afternoon. I'd been playing with my kids and came off less than parade-like when he popped in out of the blue. I loved the ratbastard more than most ten people put together, but I'm entitled to my moods like everyone else. "It's not you, Joe," I said. "Could've been anybody." I looked around. "Hey Bill," I yelled to Bill the accountant who was across the room. "When I answer the phone WHAT?, do you take it personally?"

"No," said Bill. "But you usually answer, WHAT, JOE?"

But Joe was still hurt. Wouldn't let it go. It wasn't enough that I'd described him in a previous tale as having a penis the size of a Pepsi bottle; this last story had thrown him off the horse, and now he wanted equity, some sense of spiritual restitution. Whatever that means.

I tried to escape, but he followed me around, as if being in a crowd wasn't maddening enough. I grew really annoyed at first. Expected to have a shitty time before I went. Now I had my reason.

I moved from room to room. There weren't many people, no place to hide, no women to check out, and Joe was there at every turn. Couldn't force enough Molsons down my throat to get drunk. Not one decent distraction until I felt a piss coming on, so I excused myself from the crowd and found the john. There was Joe.

"Can I talk to you?" he asked.

"Gotta piss," I said. "Will it wait till I'm done, or would you rather join me?"

"Maybe he wants to hold it for you," said Ferg, who was coming out.

"Please talk to me when you're done," said Joe.

I shut the bathroom door, pissed out the Molsons, same consistency, washed my hands with one of those little seashell soaps, dried them, then opened the door. Joe was still there.

"I surrender," I said. I promised not to write about him anymore. Never. Not if they tortured me with bamboo shoots under my fingernails or by reciting rhyming poetry or that other drivel you find in most of the little magazines; not if they tied me down and pressed my balls flat with a hot iron. Not another word.

Not even about the time when he was still with that whore June and she disappeared for a weekend and then admitted she'd been shacked up with an old boyfriend. Luckily, when she phoned Joe, it was from her parents' house. Lucky for her. No telling what he would have done if he'd been in the room when she confessed.

As it was, he ran outside barefoot in February, hopped into his Ford pick-up, drove balls-to-the-floor through town, through two red lights, down June's block, into her parents' driveway, and clean over her new '84 Trans Am. Parked right smack on top of it and cut the engine. It must have been beautiful.

I didn't see it. June's father did, though, from his comfortable perch on his plush sofa there in his living room. He leaped up, dropped his *TV Guide*, and went for Joe as Joe barged into the house hell-bent for leather. June's old man threw himself at the advancing Rambo, but Joe was too quick for him, too righteous—flipped the fat old guy straight over his back and onto the plush sofa.

Joe took the stairs two at a time. At the top, he whipped around the banister and kicked open her bedroom door with both feet. There she was, still in her nightie, the pink frilly one Joe liked, lots of leg showing, looking as good as ever. She was sprawled on her bed, phone in one hand, cigarette in the other, talking to the old boyfriend, presumably.

When she saw Joe, she got a sick look on her face like she'd swallowed bad paste.

Joe ripped the phone out of the wall, crushed it with his bare hands, threw it to the ground. He took her cigarette and ate it. Then he tossed her over his shoulder and headed back down the stairs. Hard to say where he was heading—by the time he made it out the front door, the cops had arrived.

There were two cops: A big one and a small one. Joe put June down when he saw them, marched over, gave the big one a boot in the head, hip-checked the little one into the squad car, then lifted June, who was kicking and screaming, back over his shoulder. But the kicked cop was able to crawl to his car and radio for reinforcements.

They were there within moments, cherries flashing, sirens howling. One leaped out of the squad car when he saw Joe, drew his gun, said, "Stop or I'll shoot!" What a rush that must have been.

Joe put June down again, picked up a rock, spun around and tossed it, knocking the gun out of the cop's hand. Then he charged the squad car. The cops didn't stand a chance. With little effort, Joe grabbed the vehicle by its bumper and flipped it over. It rolled three times before stopping. Then, before more reinforcements could arrive, he ran as fast and furious as he could, forgetting about the girl, realizing there were plenty more, stripping off his costume as he ran, the utility belt, the spandex pants, the cape, the shirt with the gold emblazed "J" in the middle.

By the time he got to town, Joe was down to his underpants. He looked good. He had a penis the size of a Pepsi bottle. He jumped into the first dumpster he saw, covered himself with wet garbage, and squatted there all night long, formulating a plan. Or maybe that's another story.

After a while, they blend. But that's life for you.

What can you do about it?

BEST KOREAN MASSAGE

Dave answered on the third ring.

"how can you tell when a massage is more than a massage?" I asked.

"is this a riddle?" he answered.

"hell no," I said. "there's this ad in the paper. says BEST KOREAN MASSAGE: GRAND OPENING. so I called up. they're right in Murrayville."

"interesting."

"girl sounded really cute on the phone. but I guess they all do. she gave me directions. fifty bucks for one hour."

"steep."

"yeah, but if it's more than a massage… how can you tell?"

"can't. not until you get there. either way, offer her a twenty dollar tip. you'll get what you want."

"fifty plus twenty, huh? that's serious."

"too rich for my blood. twenty for head is reasonable."

"but there's no guarantee with the fifty?"

"nope. but you can always ask, 'what do I get for a twenty dollar tip?'"

"see how inexperienced I am?"

"at least you know who to ask."

it was at #9 Jefferson Street. lots of dead businesses, especially after dark. poor Jefferson. if he only knew what they'd named after him.

#9. I found it easily enough. a two-floor walk up to a one-way-mirror glass door. a hand-written sign said ring the buzzer. I rang it. after a minute, I heard someone unlock the door. I was greeted by a pretty Asian girl—Korean, I assumed—in a tight t-shirt and short shorts. she was about five-foot tall, petite and pretty, with nice breasts and good legs. all smiles. "come in," she said. I did.

"you have appointment?"

"no. I called earlier for directions."

"oh! I spoke to you." she had a very high voice, very cute and Oriental. but I couldn't concentrate. something smelled rancid. I'd caught it the minute I walked through the door and it was getting worse. I knew it was bad manners but I had to ask. "what's that smell?"

"oh!" she giggled. "that *kimchee*."

"oh," I said, nodding my head.

"you know *kimchee*?"

"read about it in a story."

she giggled again. "it smell bad but it very good. you try?"

I curled my nose. "no thanks." I looked around. nice place. "so you're the, uh, therapist?"

"oh no! I receptionist. therapist with customer."

"can I meet her first?"

"you like see her?"

for fifty bucks, you're damn straight I like see her. I nodded. she called out something in Korean, which I didn't understand. I could only say side-kick and front-punch and count to ten. I assumed she was telling the girl to hustle it up.

"she almost done. five more minute. you sit, okay?"

"okay."

"I spray."

"come again?"

"I spray. make go away *kimchee* smell. okay?"

"okay."

I dropped onto a couch, picked up a stack of magazines on the table in front of me. *New Jersey Monthly. Time. TV Guide.* what kind of clip joint was this? I'd expected the girls to be sitting around on the couch. some variety. one from column A and one from column B.

I watched her move around the room with the aerosol can, spraying here and there. she had wonderful legs. she looked at me and giggled, very girlish. I was sorry she wasn't the masseuse.

"fifty bucks," I mumbled.

"sorry?" she stopped spraying and looked at me.

"you said on the phone fifty dollars for one hour."

"fifty for one hour," she repeated with a nod.

"how about a half hour?"

"half hour?" she thought about it. "hour is fifty. half hour is thirty-five."

"that's some math," I said. but I was happy. who the hell needs a full hour? I almost asked for the ten-minute rate. "this your place?"

"no. I just receptionist."

"how long you been in this country?"

"how long? three year."

"hmm."

"how long you here?"

"all my life."

"oh! many generation. where from?"

"Rockaway."

"oh! you Polish?"

couldn't imagine how she got that. "no," I said. "Irish, Scottish, and Apache Indian."

"oh! not Polish."

"not Polish." I was starting to think she was.

she sat down on the table in front of me, crossed those great legs magically. her thighs were looking better and better. "Irish is called Paddy," she said. "right?"

"guess so," I said.

"Paddy. I read about Irish in book. I like history very much. I read this—" she picked up the *Time*.

"is that right?" I took off my Marines cap and ran my hand through my hair.

she looked at the cap. "you soldier?"

"no. my brother gave me this."

"I see hat many time in Korea. soldier come down street many time. have affair with Korean girl. girl make pregnant, have baby, but soldier go home. sometime baby grow up and come to America if soldier remember."

"is that right?" I said.

"yes. I have cousin who is this way. her father is American soldier and her mother Korean. she very pretty. very, very pretty. this is nice mix, American and Korean."

I'd been alternating between those terrific thighs. was ready to mix a little myself. "you know," I said, "I expected to see a bunch of girls on the couch."

"really?"

"my brother took me to a massage place when I was a kid, and that's the way they did it. you went in and picked the girl you wanted."

"oh! that whore house."

"really?"

"yes. that whore house."

"well how do you like that!"

"your brother bring you there? you how old?"

"twelve or fourteen."

"oh!"

I put my cap back on. "a whore house," I said. "well I'll be hog-tied." but I wasn't. I was out on the street, turning the corner, looking for a bar to drop my fifty dollars in.

Giving the Finger

It was just the tip of my finger, my pinkie, and when I describe it that way it doesn't sound like much, but there it was, hanging quietly, bent over like a broken soldier. and that's how I thought of it. a soldier. just a pinkie, sure, but we'd been through hell together for thirty-six years, which is longer than most marriages last. and I was angry again: at myself for not keeping a solid fist when I threw that punch; at the universe for conspiring against me, sniping at me, picking off another limb, a piece of my life and leaving it lifeless, pathetic. I can respect the shark baring down at me, teeth bared, ferocious, all cartilage and appetite, but there's something godrotten about being nibbled to death.

I'd won the first two fights, more or less. survival is winning—survival without a crippling injury. nothing to brag about considering the opponents, but it beats losing. the first, an eighteen-year-old purple belt with blond curls and bad acne, throwing reverse after reverse punch, predictable, but look who's talking.

the second guy was tougher. a brown belt nearing his *shodan*, a handsome, nineteen-year-old gentleman named Steve. I'd seen him before and liked him, his style, manner. seemed like a stand-up guy. he'd been training with my teacher for six years, been kicked around and busted up by some mean mother blackbelts and had gotten up each time with that smooth Vermont grin and soft eyes that said thank you, sir, may I have another? and they'd knocked him down again and again. Steve. I respected him. still a kid, but he was all heart. good upbringing, no doubt, and trained by the best. Sensei was the best. six straight years. how I envied him: nearly half my age and calm, poised. no savagery. I'd have broken his back in any barroom, but I held back, played by the rules: no face shots, no groin, no knees, kidneys, just speed tag to the target zone, ineffective roundhouse kicks to the chest and other clean point scores. I'd detested sports karate when I trained at his age, knew the bad habits it formed, and here I was playing patty cake, looking for the cheap points. caught him once with a hard one to the breadbasket and he winced and I felt sorry—then he grinned smooth and calm. thank you, sir, may I have another?

I'd lost it. they called me sensei now, too, those students of mine, but it was an empty word at this moment. I was part of the system, part of the problem, taking it easy on everyone, careful not to hurt them, playing speed tag when I should be fighting. and here, 250 miles from home, here in front of *my* sensei, the *real* sensei, I was a joke, and I knew it, and that's what really hurt.

so I suppose I was aware of what was coming next, somewhere deep in the bowels of my subconscious. I needed a good lesson and it was coming my way whether I liked it or not. deserves ain't got nothing to do with it. that's just the way it is, the way things go, the way the universe conspires, sets you up, knocks you down, taking small bites from time to time and reserving true judgment for the real warriors, the true *bushidos*, those bad enough to die well while the rest of us fake it with belts and certificates and awards and half friends and trophy wives and corporate vice presidencies and stock portfolios and Kehoe accounts and BMWs and TV shows we can't miss and season tickets to inane spectacles and empty parties and hair weaves and membership at health clubs and John Grisham novels and golf and video games and shit and more shit, and heart attacks, low humor, empty heroics, meaningless death.

feh. give me the shark. bring on the motherfucker.

Sensei was only my height, which isn't much, and he was old enough to be my father. and he had grandkids. and he was losing his hair and some of his teeth. but none of that matters. a shark is a shark. I knew that I didn't have a chance and that it was for my own good. didn't matter. I froze in terror as he removed his tattered belt and tied it around my left leg and then around his.

"how are you going to fight now?" he asked and his eyes laughed.

I looked at my leg tied to his. nowhere to run. no fancy spinning back kicks. no flash. no bullshit. just my fists and head, whatever was left of it. just me and myself. tied to a shark.

he didn't throw any punches. didn't have to. I was frozen and he knew it. defeated just like that. didn't even give it my best shot, but a half-assed one, hand open and flying at him, which he blocked with that steel mallet he calls a fist. and I felt the snap. the pinkie was gone. and that was that.

I sat in the surgeon's office two days later, Vermont 250 miles behind me, nursing a shattered ego, which would eventually repair itself, even if the pinkie didn't. I already knew what the doctor would say. this one's a write-off, kid. this little piggy went home. feel thankful it's not something worse.

thankful. oh yeah. thankful and mother dumb.

the price paid for living on the edge, stepping over the line every once in a while to see how it feels, dangling without benefit of sense or a parachute. giving life the finger.

End of the World News

My left arm hurt so badly that I hadn't slept more than a little. should've taken a pain killer, Tylenol, something, but didn't, just let the bastard throb, my head tossing on the pillow. everyone suffers, why shouldn't I?

I was depressed, too, which was nothing new, but this time I had reason, which was. goddamn arm. popped out of the joint when I was tossing the kid around. wondered if I needed another operation. it was barely a year since the last one, that $13,000 knee they rebuilt, which still went out of joint from time to time. couldn't get much for $13,000 these days, end of the world and all. the way it was going, we'd need AK-47s just to get in and out of ShopRite soon. the Dow peeking at 6,800, setting new records every other week. everyone fat and complacent and thinking it wouldn't stop, historically deprived idiots, no sense of gravity, as in what goes up— but I didn't give a rat's ass. just wanted my arm back. the apocalypse was coming. can't swing a broad sword with one arm.

got to work late. told the receptionist that I'd been calling the doctor all morning and was still waiting for a callback, waiting for him to "allow" me to get an MRI. dumb fuck had to take his pound of flesh before moving me on to a specialist. insurance rules. end-of-the-world rules.

a letter from Israel beamed in from my e-mail server. it was from my friend Marty, a religious guy who used to smoke a lot of grass and then lost his hand in a cutting machine while working at a factory and became religious. If I forget you, O Jerusalem, let my right hand forget its dexterity. some guys take that stuff seriously. especially at the end of the world.

>Thursday, January 23, 1997 01:27:34
>
>You asked how things are. Well, here's a cheery bit of news. Pray for us.
>
>Marty
>
>(attached)
>
>A U.S. Congressional Task Force report warns that Syria, Iran, Iraq, and the Palestinian Authority are cooperating in preparation for war with

Israel. Syrian President Assad and Saddam Hussein of Iraq met secretly to this end in the spring of 1996. Other secret meetings have been held between the Syrian government and the Palestinian Authority, including agreements that the Palestinian police and other "armed elements" will cause "flare-ups in the Israeli interior in case of an escalation in the north." This is the first media revelation of the report, although it was released last month.

Congressman Jim Saxton (R, N.J.), who heads the Task Force on Terrorism and Unconventional Warfare, said that the American Administration is making a mistake in not relating to the possibility of a break-out of war in the Middle East with more seriousness. Saxton said, "Because the American people want to hear that the peace process is succeeding, it becomes less difficult for the administration to brush aside possible threats to Israel, rather than deal with them directly.... According to this report, there is a clear and present danger to Israel and the Israeli people. By watching the policies of the former Israeli government and the current policies of the U.S. government, one would think that things are just wonderful and that we have nothing to worry about in the Middle East, and all we have to do is make agreements like Hevron and everything will work out fine. But those of us in this Congressional Task Force believe the facts that are presented in this report...and that the Clinton administration should recognize that the reality may not be the same as it would prefer to see..."

"Numerous sources in the region report that the supreme leaders in most Arab states, as well as in Iran and Pakistan, are convinced that the present vulnerability of Israel is so great that there is a unique opportunity to begin the process leading to the destruction of Israel. These circumstances are considered to be a historic window of opportunity the Muslim world should not miss. Toward this end, several Arab states, as well as Iran and Pakistan, have been engaged in a frantic military build-up and active preparations in the last few months..."

I couldn't concentrate on the report. Morgenstern was in his cube, raving and drooling. he'd just read Aryat 7, which always gave him rabies. he was so loud that I couldn't hear myself think, so I went over to drink my coffee to his cacophony.

"...even the leftists, those stinking *Meretz* who killed right-wing Jews, even they wouldn't have gone this far. give over Hevron? give away your father's burial place? Golda Meir would puke if she saw this! Ben Gurian would shit his pants!"

"I'm so depressed, I can't think," I said.

"depressed? c'mon, man—the apocalypse is good for guys like us. this is the best news. it's all prophecy. Gog and Magog."

"I'm depressed about my arm," I said. "can't straighten it. I don't give a damn about those cowards. you reap what you sow."

"you *do* give a shit, which is why you're depressed."

"can't swing a sword with one arm."

"to hell with swords. give me a grenade launcher. I won't be happy until I smell burnt flesh; crisp, charred—"

I went back to my cube, coffee cold, peeled open a candy bar. called the doctor's office again. Patel, Patel and Patel. got the receptionist.

"this is my fourth call," I said. "I don't need an appointment. just give me an authorization number so I can get an MRI."

"we can't do that," she said. "Dr. Patel needs to see you first."

"it's an old karate accident," I said. "tore some ligaments. I've been through this before. all I need is the MRI to see how bad it is."

"we can't do that. Dr. Patel needs to see you first," she repeated. at least I think it was a she. could have been a recording. either way, there was no point arguing. I hung up and pulled out the keyboard and began to type.

"Dear Marty—

Besides praying, what are you doing? Aren't any of your leaders taking responsibility for protecting you folks by whatever means necessary? Or have the last of them been jailed? Where are your 'rabbis' now? Why isn't Shach screaming about this instead of the Lubavitcher Rebbe? I don't get it, pal. These last few moves have been suicidal, and while I respect suicide, I wouldn't go like that—*kosherous*, t'fillin, trappings and drippings. I'm so depressed that all I can do is eat candybars and drink coffee and pretend for five minutes here and there that it's not real. Don't think I can stomach being a Jew like our parents' generation, bemoaning the hitlers, taking my kids to the Museum of the Second Holocaust—

If I didn't have children, I can see going over there and killing as many of those cocksuckers as possible before the end-game and there's no one left to kill. I'm about *this* close."

but who was I kidding? armchair warrior. fucked-up arm. couldn't swing a broad sword. fat, complacent American. exquisitely bored, just like all the rest.

excuses are like assholes; everyone has one and they all stink.

in the next cube, I could hear Errol chiding Morgenstern. Errol, salesman, ex-basketball player, ex-socialist, ex-Black Muslim, current Baptist, current conservative. so it goes. he smelled the wound and brought salt. everyone's a vicious bastard at the end of the world.

"so what do you think of the Hevron deal?" he asked. as if he cared. but that didn't matter. I could feel the blood drain out of Morgenstern's face. he tore Errol a new asshole, which is convenient if you're in prison, it occurs to me. end-of-the-world humor.

"how long do you think Israel could survive without the rest of the world?"

"they could go back to eating sardines with pride!" said Morgenstern. "they could live without Pepsi and Burger King. but no—they want to be Americans!"

I was trying to work, trying to write, but nothing made sense. went to scratch my back and almost keeled over. arm kicked like a mule. I was sick to my gut. end-of-the-world pains.

then I remembered a dream Buk had, or maybe it was a poem. he was on a plane, having a drink, staring at this stewardess's terrific legs. suddenly there was tremendous turbulence. then an engine blew. real loud explosion. everyone panicked as face-masks popped out all over the depressurized cabin. the pilot screamed over the p.a. to stay calm, but it was obvious—that sucker was going *down*. Buk knew he had about 90 seconds until impact, so he worked fast: grabbed the stewardess from behind, pulled up her skirt and stuck it in; kept ramming it home, ramming it home, as the plane plummeted all the way to the ground.

as I sat in Dr. Patel's office sniffing curry, I read the newspaper: a bomb explosion in D.C. had taken out an abortion clinic leaving three dead and four wounded; two wealthy teenagers from New Jersey had stuffed their newborn down a toilet; O.J. Simpson was about to walk away clean.

my arm throbbed, teeth hurt, head about to explode. the end of the goddamn world. and me without a stewardess.

PART THREE

UNDER-TURE

eulogy for dead poems

the disk crashed, taking bits and bytes and
six of my poems,
and I had no backups, no hard copy,
nothing.
just this eulogy and shame.
I live with shame.
the force that thru the green fuse
drives the flower, drives my shame,
gives me poems, takes them back.
the god that made mosquitoes, flies,
& Tommy a millionaire
& Jody's wife a plaintiff,
has taken his ball of shit
and gone home.
what fucking waste.
losing poems to electronics, bad sectors,
careless death.
I offer my life and it steals my poems.
such unholiness deserves tears, not tributes.
but as Buk observed: there's plenty of poets,
and too few poems.

UNDERTURE

Flight of the Daredevil

The Daredevil looked out on the city.
>   *This is my city,* he said to the black wind,
>   *This is my town.*
>   But the black wind was rude and blew black
>   crumbs & dead soot.
The Daredevil stared into the black wind's face
>   with blind eyes & open maw
>   & muscles taut & muscles slack
>   & broken hearted,
>   with thoughts of taking flight,
>   not swinging Tarzan-like from roofs
>   but a Hemingway swan dive with twin song
>   thru disinterested wind,
>   plummeting toward pavement
>   like a sack of ripe fruit.
>   This is my city; this is my town.

Who will bury me? Silence.
Who will mourn me? Silence.
Who will replace me? Silence.
Who is the Daredevil?
Silence.

The Daredevil contemplated his finale
>   but heard the cries below, somewhere in his city,
>   his town, and without further thought,
>   swooped hawk-like, swan-like, Daredevil-like
>   to a destiny calling—
>   to something in trouble: man, woman, child;
>   to Silence
>   & black wind.
>   my city. my town.
>   Through hunger & the needle

he peered into the darkness
seeking the goddess of verisimilitude;
but the darkness had raped her,
disassembled her and eaten her children.
      (we hate our children.)

I will not surrender, screamed the Daredevil,
    but the wind laughed and he heard it
    & muscles tensed again as he swung down to
    a destiny calling;
    no swan dive nor swan song,
    a good night to die,
    but better to live—
    the only Fuck You he could afford.

UNDERTURE

a miracle of modern medicine

he was an amateur drunk, I guess,
the way he ran the light,
jumped the curb,
crashed through the mailbox,
and plowed into me.

I was on the lawn, suddenly,
thrown by the force of the crash.
couldn't feel my legs.
everything spinning.

a crowd gathered.

I heard noises.
screaming.
finally, an ambulance.

two men in white coats
stood over me.
EMS workers.
one asked me if I could talk.

"yes."

"do you know your name?"

"yes."

"don't try to move.
we're taking you to the
hospital."

"which one?" I asked.

"Memorial," he said.
"it's just a mile from here."

"I'm not sure if my insurance covers service at that hospital," I said.
"and you'd better contact my primary care physician first.
he'll authorize the service or refer you to a specialist.
then the specialist will authorize the hospital visit.
he's a nice man, the doctor. Indian, I think. barely speaks English.
I don't know if he's a good doctor or not, but he was the only name
on my plan within a twenty-five miles radius of where I live.
his name is Patel.
I'd appreciate if you'd hurry.
I think I'm bleeding to death."

who by fire

Rosh Hashanah's
gray rain & dark skies—
bad for traffic.

the dead push forward,
languid, slow,
toward the dead jobs
that killed them.
bankers, programmers, salesmen—
young upwardly mobile dead.

who by mergers? who by down-sizing?

I fight the crowd,
cut off a zombie in
my Toyota.
the meek shall inherit
nothing.
weave, rage through the lemmings,
against my own
film noir destiny,
these evil dead,
but…

I slow up at the sight of
the orange neon poncho
of a cop writing tickets.

who by summons?
better you than me, brother.

Shabbos Tshuvah

so it was the day before Yom Kippur,
the Day of Atonement,
and I was in *shul* looking hard
for something to feel guilty about.
well, I was late, so that was something,
and I was angry, but that's something else.
I was angry because there were two Lubavitchers
sitting there,
with their special Lubavitch prayer books in
their special Lubavitch laps.
I'd come to hate their black coats, expensive hats,
cheap shoes, bad breath,
their sanctimonious insistence that
the Rebbe was the messiah
or *wasn't* the messiah,
depending on which side of the schism they were on.
these two were *Meshichists*,
radiant, smug,
a perfect pair—
a recovering alcoholic desperate for the approval of a rabbi,
and a recovering cokehead, frantic to be regarded as a rabbi.
two assholes.
in my *shul*.
the day before Yom Kippur.
I couldn't wait to get home and
throw down a beer.

the real rabbi—whatever *that* means—
stood up to make his speech.
I stood up too,
walked outside into the sun and air,
September air, clean and cool.
children played across in the park,

laughing,
better than any speech, but then
silence is better.
finally, it ended.
everyone walked outside in their suits, dresses,
smiling, chattering, self-forgiving.
I turned to go home
but the rabbi stopped me.
asked if I'd make it back by six o'clock.
"there's never have enough men for afternoon services,"
I said. "what's the occasion?"

"the Lubavitchers don't have anywhere to go today,"
he said.

"sorry," I said,
though I wasn't.

I walked away alone,
stopped by a friend's house for a beer, had 2,
went home, had 4 more,
then went back to shul.
I walked down the street,
head high like Gary Cooper.

Ralph the *mesuginah* slept in a pew.
I listened to him snore for a moment, then
went to the bookshelf,
gathered up all the Lubavitch prayer books,
tossed them in a box,
then dragged them down into the basement
and threw them into a dark corner.
go make bricks without straw.

then I walked back upstairs and
waited for them to arrive,
waited for them to search high and low
like children for an *afikoman*,
waited there drunk and raw
hoping one of them would say something,
demand something,
try some anger,
yank my chain,
make me do something I'd regret,
take a swing at a face,
make me scream,
BECAUSE YOU KILLED HIM, YOU FUCKERS!
you killed him and you killed me, too.

I stood there sick,
drawing heavy breaths,
a Jew without a beard
staring out the window for a half-dozen
beards without Jews.

this is a lousy poem
and I am a lousy poet,
and not a very good Jew either, it seems.
but it's almost Yom Kippur,
and in another hour,
I'll
be
sorry.

2 nuns

it was a party for one of Roger's kids,
I don't know which one.
they'd just baptized him or something pagan.
I got there late.

"come up on the porch," said Rog. "too many bugs out here."
"you'd have *eaten* the bugs in the old days," I said.
Rog laughed. "yeah. the good old days."

on the porch, faces I hadn't seen in years.
friends of friends. Roger's relatives.
his grandmother kissed me,
her whiskers on mine.
his mom had gotten fatter. who hadn't?
I drank Shlitz, chewed Skoal.
Then the jokes began.
I told the one about 2 nuns instructed by the
mother superior to paint the convent and not get their
habits dirty. so they decide to do it in the buff.
suddenly, there's a knock on the door.
"blind man," says a voice.
the 2 nuns shrugged; what's the harm?
one opened the door.
"nice tits, sister," said the guy. "where do you want these blinds?"
more Shlitz. more Skoal.
Roger's brother Al shot off fireworks, making some of
the littler kids cry.
just like the old days.
then this fat drunken bitch who was dating one of Roger's pals
saw me and screamed, "is that Meth? that sonuvabitch
stabbed my brother in high school—"
I was glad I was already leaving.
heard she spoiled it for everyone.

2 beds

"whose bed is this?" my son asked.

"oh—anybody can sleep here.
do *you* want to sleep here?"

"no," said my boy.

my father smiled,
then lurked about the room,
looking for something, pushing aside
piles of magazines thick with dust,
odd bits of TV sets, radio parts.
"ah," he said at last,
finding it tucked in a brown paper bag.
he left the room with it—
left me alone with my boy.

I looked at the bed.
anybody's.
he'd always slept there alone
in his office, his "den."
this embarrassed me, of course,
especially that time I was eleven,
and Bruce Partnoy, who was sleeping over,
asked, "why doesn't he sleep with
your mother?"

bad back,
I said.

my father, 84, called me to the TV room.
I entered.
used to be *my* room.

had matching desk & dresser, then,
hi-fi, Beatles 8-tracks, blacklight, beanbag chair,
nerf-ball hoop, incense burner, cactus plants,
Ellison books, Nietzsche, *Bhagavad Gita*,
an Iron Man poster, another of Che,
my own 12-in TV, the smell of pot, a small blue rug,
a box of rubbers—
now it was *his* room.
no plants. no posters.
no trace of me.
a *different* blue rug; a *different* TV.
diplomas.
the smell of Vick's and dust and death.

"c'mere," he said.
he reached into the brown bag,
withdrew a toy from inside,
a fuzzy weasel attached to a ball.
"turn it on. it chases the ball.
the kids will think it's terrific."

"it'll scare the baby,"
I said.

"no it won't."

he fiddled with the batteries for
long moments.
painfully.
insisted I learn how.
"this side is positive," he said,
"and this side—"
I stared at his diplomas—

an E.E. from CCNY,
an M.E. from Dayton.
now he couldn't field a battery.
proof of God, I thought.
randomness does not do this to a man.

downstairs, the children played
with my old skateboard.
there was hardly any floor space;
a ping-pong table cut the room in half—
hadn't been played on in decades,
but still there,
vaguely green beneath gray-white dust,
a workbench now to screws & bolts & circuit boards,
color-coded, size-ordered, meticulously organized in dust.
one of the children slipped
and the board flew into the glass doors
with a thud
but nothing broke.

Bruce Partnoy became a dentist.
friends say he's still an asshole.

I heard my father calling from upstairs,
asking me to help fix the closet door.
"off the caster again," he said.
I used to kick it off.
he brought out his flashlight,
the one with two bulbs that he'd had
for 30 years.
offered to hold the door for me,
but I refused.
would rather work alone, I said.
don't need any help.

learned *that* from him, too.
help meant criticism.
learned to live without praise
and suppose I should be grateful.
to work alone, breathe alone—

cut your own goddamn lawn.
I'll get a car without your help.
I don't need you.
fuck you.

grateful.
I heard the children downstairs;
far away.
safe.
inevitably, he leads me to the drawer
for the dreaded ritual.
he locked it tight when I was a child,
but that magic drawer was
no longer secret.
bank books, stock certificates,
bonds.

"do we *have* to go through this again?"
I asked.

"you should know just in case."

I looked away

just in case
death.

I've lived with it as long as I can remember—
since the first heart attack,

the second,
the stroke, the memories, nightmares—
the moods I mimic and despise.

but you don't die.

you make me live 10,000 deaths,
my guilt at hating you,
worshipping you,
screaming at you,
screaming *like* you—

but not 2 beds.

at night,
I curl up beside my gift,
careful not to wake her,
content to hear her breathing,
hug sheets she's warmed,
cry real tears,
eat troughs of regret,
fistfuls 'til sick,
alone, but never 2 beds.

I share your face, old man—
not your crimes, but mine,
write letters you won't read,
poems,
but mark no more excuses
for you or myself
behind Siamese masques

and the 10,000 deaths
I inherit.

parking spot

she.
was.
exquisite.

perfect, actually.
I spotted her walking
as I pulled into the lot.
every so often a woman like this
falls from the sky,
radiating,
cast out perhaps,
but to hell with politics.

from behind the wheel,
I watched her walk,
stop at the intersection,
cross.
her hair, legs,
angelic ass
entered the department store.

I looked around the lot,
but nothing.
I circled the rows and rows
of parked cars,
cursing, praying,
desperate to find something quickly,
but nothing,
nothing…
and then—

eureka!
up ahead, a real tight spot

between 2 Jap cars—
a Honda and a Ford.
as I pulled forward,
a horn blew LOUD.
I looked up and this shmuck
in a Hyundai rolled down his window.

UNDERTURE

"I was waiting for that spot!"
he said.
"oh?" I said,
pulling in.
the meek shall inherit
nothing.

I got out, bolted across the street,
through the door,
entered the department store and
looked around.
it had only been 2 minutes,
but she was nowhere in sight.
I wasn't discouraged, though—
the advantage of
nothing to lose.

I hunted.
checked the make-up counter,
dresses,
lingerie.

finally found her in shoes,
looking at pumps.
that angelic ass
monolithic,
motionless.

I was motionless, too,
desperate for something to say.
something different—
confident, yet subdued.
"didn't I see you in

last month's *Victoria's Secret Catalog*?"
no.
something. *any*thing.
didn't get the chance, though.
just at that moment, the guy from the lot
walked in.
the Hyundai guy,
smiling like he'd brushed his teeth
with piss.
he was taller than me,
better dressed.
we stared at each other.

the adrenaline was running now.
all muscles tensed.

he walked toward me,
slowly, slowly…
passed me,
went straight towards her—
clapped his hand on her ass.
she startled, then smiled.
then kissed him full on the lips.

before he could pay for
those shoes,
I was back in the lot
turning the key in my ignition.

I find, as I get older,
too many stories end
like
this.

everything I eat

all the peach yogurt,
all the hamburgers well done,
fried eggs and beef sausages
at 2 a.m.,
the curried meat pies, fried chicken,
chopped-liver on a roll with
red onion and mustard and a side of
potato salad,
the lamb-kabob from Ma'abat Steak House
on Cedar Lane,
the pizza, fries,
tortilla chips with salsa,
the Baskin Robbins chocolate-fudge ice-cream,
the candy bars,
the bread,
everything I eat turns to shit,
which is no revelation,
but I'd rather *eat* that shit
than the shit they print in those poetry magazines
that editors ask me to subscribe to.

Cigarettes

his wife finally left the porch, went upstairs
& he lit one.

"those things are going to kill you," I said.
but he didn't care, or acted like he didn't.
blew the smoke out with relief.
"thought you quit," I said.

"did," he said. "you scared me straight."
blew puffs of death at me,
not rude, but close enough to smell.

"so when did you start again?"

"2 weeks ago, when my father-in-law died.
had to watch the body until someone came to relieve me."

he sucked the cigarette like a teat; milk-white smoke
plumed from his nostrils. "gonna quit again. get in shape.
want to get up and ride bikes in the morning?
5 a.m.?"

"you nuts?" I said. "I write 'til 1:00 or 2:00."

just then, his wife came downstairs and
screamed at him—screamed like I wasn't even there.
her hair was in a kerchief. no make-up.
her skin, the color of a police photograph.
crows feet. looked like hell. hell screaming.

"I'm sorry," I said when she left again.

"for what?"

"smoke all you want."

horse sense

they caught him when he fell off the bucket.
he'd been standing on it because of
the height differential
and it worked.

the newspaper said he'd been employed at the track stables;
that he snuck in after hours and chained the mare
so she couldn't move,
then dropped his pants,
climbed up on the bucket,
and stuck it in her.

the next day at his arraignment,
he could have denied it—
even with the evidence,
he could have said the cops held him down,
jerked him off,
and planted his sperm in the horse.
after all, it worked for O.J.

but he didn't.
he pleaded guilty.

when the judge asked him why he did it,
he said he couldn't afford a hooker.

I was angered when I read this.
imagine,
the ego of the man,
thinking that somehow he could
satisfy a horse.

the yahrtzeit of my knee

100 fights,
give or take;
the price paid
for a wise mouth
& quick temper.

black eyes,
busted lips,
a hairline fracture in one rib,
chipped elbow with a floater,
chipped teeth,
concussions,
but the knees held up.

until last year.

one lousy accident
(it's always an accident)
snapped the ACL,
tore the meniscus,
then 5 hours under the knife.
Morphine,
Percocets,
alcohol & marijuana,
guilt and resolutions
broken;
a fiber ligament,
two surgical screws
and a bill I'm still paying.

35 years into baby fat
with one fall.

now,
one year,
260 hours of stretching,
$13,000 murdered,
an 8,000-word novella;
and it still hurts.
like a motherfucker.

yisgadal, v'yiskadash sh'may rabo.

the black eye

he had punched another boy,
an older boy, and been sent home.
was waiting at the door
when I arrived.

"let's walk," I said.

he was worried.
thought I'd be angry when
I learned of the black eye.
but I wasn't.
especially when I heard
the story—

the older boy had hurt his friend,
twisted an arm behind his back,
making the littler kid
cry.
so my boy popped him.

popping bullies runs in the family,
I told him.

we walked & walked.
it was brisk, autumn,
red and brown leaves
piled on the side of the road.
he'd have jumped in them
a few years ago, I thought.
not now.

we took the long way around.
he threw acorns at trees,

UNDERTURE

asked about the stock market.
9 years old.
just yesterday I held him,
cradled,
bottles and diapers—
9.
already getting into
fist fights.
girls would be next.

we've all run down this
gush.
sunrise, sunset.
I always hated it
but now it's me,
my child,
and it hurts.
hurts like any black eye,

wonderfully.

for Avi

the circus

bravo.
bravo depression.
bravo amphetamine—

1:30 am,
another sleepless Monday smear
which began when I coughed up $360
for Itzhak Perlman tickets
I couldn't afford,
then watched Netscape all day
hoping a stock I owned would move
so I could pay for the tickets
(it moved down),
an afternoon worrying because
my boss was bitchy from the acid
he'd dropped Sunday, which he called Ecstasy,
which wasn't.
an evening watching bad film, bad TV,
some allusion to Abraham's willingness
to sacrifice his son—
so pious, righteous,
a true theologian (but who'd want him for a father?)
then "Bewitched" in black & white,
Darren losing his job but
forbidding Samantha to use her powers.
the schmuck.

there's 2 things I've learned—
USE YOUR POWERS
& when the circus comes to town, GO!
life's too short not to see Itzhak Perlman.

1:45. stuffed with nachos

& Drakes
poison,
suffering through a poetry magazine
some idiot begged me to buy.
should've just given her the money,
but I opened it,
watched it leak out.
the best effort: an over-baked turd about
some guy fucking a spider's asshole,
then downhill. fast.

and *my* stuff keeps coming back.

cripples

we ate quickly and left the office,
me driving.
Morgenstern wanted to stop at the bank,
but I pulled up at a bar,
right next to a handicap spot.

"what are you doing?"
he asked.

"getting a beer," I said.
"wait here if you want."

several later, I felt better.
Morgenstern and I talked about women,
the ones around the office,
the ones we'd sleep with,
or wouldn't.
he had more tolerance than I,
but that's age for you.
after a certain point,
even pretty men start
looking good.

he had another beer.
began talking about business,
making plans,
beer plans that would come to
nothing.

I looked at my watch—
our lunch hour spent,
and my cash.
I paid and we left.

outside,
I got into my car
as someone pulled up beside me.
I rolled down my window.

"excuse me, sir—
you can't park there."

"and why is that, *sir*?"
he said very snotty.

"because it's a handicap spot,"
I said.

he ignored me.
stormed off indignant
into the bar.

I just sat there for a moment.

and then I felt it.
adrenaline.
like a familiar lover.
I got out and slammed the door.

"*now* what?"
Morgenstern asked.

"he was fine,"
I said.

"so?"

"so I'm gonna cripple the
sonuvabitch."
"but he has a sticker,"
said Morgenstern. "look."

I looked.
there it was, on his windshield:
a handicap sticker.
somehow I had missed it.
I was confused.

"he wasn't even limping,"
I said.

"maybe his wife's an invalid,"
said Morgenstern.

"but she's not with him.
I'm going in."

"wait!" he said.
"think about it—
he's humping a cripple.
how good can *that* be?
he *deserves* to park there."

I halted,
thought about that for a moment,
turned around,
& got back in the car.

fairies

my kid's tooth fell out,
his front tooth
& he ran to show me.

"look!" he said, smiling like a
jack-o'-lantern,
holding out the little white pebble
as if he'd discovered
something magical.

"that's nice," I said.

he ran away to wrap it up,
place it under his pillow.

I looked in my wallet.
the tooth fairy had bills
to pay,
and there was always
somebody with their hand out—
the tax fairy,
the power & electric fairies.

I envied my son,
still in that rose-colored world
with altruistic fairies.

thought about that again
later on the toilet—
it struck me as I stared
into the pot.

the turd fairy.
man—I'd be rich!

pizza

it had been a long night,
horrible, endless,
the wife trying to assure me I wasn't alone,
me trying to assure me,
cold sweat,
dripping thoughts of suicide utopia;
no drugs to blame,
bad chemistry, perhaps,
bad programming—

the morning was easier.
the morning had sun and work and
children to tend—

I listened to Bach as I scrambled eggs,
mixed chocolate milk, popped toast.
my son tore the top off a cereal box,
said he was saving them for a
Captain Crunch telescope.
I had that once, I thought.

the baby needed changing,
a deep brown smear.
decided to bathe him,
keep him quiet,
let the wife get the sleep we'd
both missed.
I got into the tub with him,
hugged his wet body,
washed his hair, his fatty arms & legs,
him jabbering all the while,
unknown words,
but a few made it through:

daddy, bath, pizza.

"too early for pizza," I said.

"pizza! pizza!" he screamed,
and I screamed, too—
he'd grabbed my balls.

"that's *penis*," I said.
"not pizza. and don't bother mine.
you have your own."

"oh," he said.

I smiled and swirled the water.
he smiled and swirled the water.

I sighed.
he sighed.

he had my face;
same hair, same mouth—
my face with an eternal light.
I had that once, I thought.

"you're not alone,"
I told him, hoping it
would stick.

then I opened the drain
and let the water
run
out.

by request

we left the bar around midnight
still sober enough to drive.
everyone shook hands
& went their separate ways
except Tommy, who offered to drive
me to my car.

"it's just over there," I said, pointing,
but he insisted.
went 3 blocks out of his way
around a one-way circle.

"you never write about me,"
he said.

I played with his car phone,
sat back in the plush leather of his Cadillac.
"you're not a character,"
I answered, apologetically.
"take Joe—you can talk about him
all night. running over his girlfriend's
car with his 4-by-4;
spending the night in a dumpster—"

Tommy checked his Rolex.
"you think my life is easy?"

"hell no," I said.
I checked my Rolex, too.
discovered I didn't have one.
then got out and walked to
my Cadillac.
but I didn't have one of those
either.
just these 147 words.

million man death

Bert & Ernie on childhood TV
promised Laurel & Hardy adulthood, but
Bert ended up a Republican.

Farrakhan on Death TV
wants my fear
       (me, white jew god,
       prostrate to fear?)
Luftwaffing that
all blacks hate
whites,
all women hate
MEN
but I'm not fooled—
women don't hate me
until they've had me.

I sit in front of 19-inch
400-pixel death,
like Valens
watching the Goths come
over the hill,
mouths frothing,
needing a beer,
set to destroy a Rome
they couldn't build.

I fear them as any white,
fat & lazy as any Roman
jew, whose pitiful lack of
congregate faith has borne decline
& the rending of garments
& sackcloth & ash.

I fear a world without Ernies,
a planet of home boys.
me.
middle-class thirty-something
white american jew goy,
crawling under the nearest rock
to wait,
as the ruthless inherit the world,
and the white inherits his fate.

and if you feel a sting,
that's just pride fucking with you.

Some relief (though not much)

I was crying
& my wife handed me a jar under the door.
it said Tucks.
pads with witch hazel
for fast temporary relief of hemorrhoids,
which is a malady of the ass.
don't cry,
she said through the door. *I've suffered, too.*
try these—
it will help.
so I did.
but it didn't help the poetry.
the rejection slips kept coming.
I just sat there and strained
knowing full well there's no jarred muses,
just maladies of the ass
& cures for everything,
except people wiping the smears of their lives
against the world.
but look who's talking.

Hairy Hands

Denville, NJ, end of summer,
gluey,
waiting for the rain or the
shit end of some hurricane,
waiting out my 1-hour lunch break in
thin jerkwater town,
½ a cheese sandwich down.

I pick up the dry cleaning,
stare at a magazine rack,
study a pair of legs, trim ankles,
digesting cheese.
it's called killing time—
terrible expression for a
terrible deed,
but that's all I had.

I try the bookstore where they've
never heard of Jeffers or Buk;
the video store but it's all
garbage.

I want a beer, but I restrain myself,
wander into a jewelry shop instead.
the owner realizes I'm just
wasting time, his & mine,
stares out the window scratching
hairy hands,
complains how the town has changed—
high rent, high taxes,
too many niggers, etc.

soon, I'm back on the sidewalk,

½ a cheese sandwich & 10 minutes
left—
I look around.
hadn't changed that much.
still jerkwater.
still cheese.

Prison gray nights

> *Death is also trying to be life*
> —Ted Hughes

I stare into the toilet before flushing.
this is something I do too often.
I've never been good at good-byes.

upstairs, she is crying,
or perhaps sick of it,
awaiting the next tremor,
and I am reminded of my mother's tears,
terrible,
those prison gray nights.

he'd slam the door invariably
and she'd wait like a fool,
praying he'd return
safe and undamaged.
she didn't know I was still awake,
staring into the black,
clutching some wretched stuffed animal,
loathing her tears and praying the opposite.

one day, my father turned his blackness
on me.
my fault, no doubt,
a sass mouth, an arrogant brow,
the weapons of youth pitting
the hot sting of leather.
his eyes were also a strap,
terrible and black.
he'd buckle me good, sometimes,
aiming higher as I grew,

the back and legs, alternately,
until one day my rage belittled his,
and I lifted a wine bottle,
swung it like a bat,
missed his head but caught the elbow
hard and brought him
down.
when he returned from the hospital,
his arm in plaster,
we didn't look at each other
for some time—
but later that evening,
I plugged in my mother's iron,
pressed it to my forearm,
a 2nd degree punishment of sorts.

I am older now.
I have friends and a wife and children.
I have a mortgage and 2-car garage.
I pay my fair share of taxes.
I have life insurance policies and a 401(k) plan.
my phone can answer itself.
I have another phone in my car.
I drive a Japanese car.
I go to work each morning.
at night, I watch videos.
other nights, I get drunk.
I go to the gym sometimes.
my joints ache when it rains.
the gutters of my house need cleaning.
I can't stand most of what I read.
the news depresses me.
many things depress me.

I fear male-pattern baldness and constipation
more than cancer.
I have a 9-mm Browning that I may
someday put to my head.
when I scream, I hear the same obscenities
my father used.

I stare into the toilet before flushing,
stare at my shit, then flush.

but it's still there.

as if it matters

1:34 a.m.
my world
asleep;
my wife, children.

outside, a cold & dark
black winter.

I write these things
as if they matter,
as if any of it,
as if
Hem or Buk
or Ellison matter;
Lennon, Cobain,
Morrison.

dead.
everything dead.

Rebbe dead
& angels dead.
my world—
the dead and
dead to be.
paint chipping,
lawn dying,
car stalling,
tooth aching.
and I write as if
it matters.
proposals by day,
poems at dusk,

like a miserable clerk,
like Kafka matters
or Dos or Jeffers.
as if anything does.
as if words were something,
anything.
nothing.

does it matter?
does it matter?
ask the dust.

UNDERTURE
Rimbaud, Bukowski, Morrison, and me

she brushes hair from my face,
this siren—
brings me yellow garlands,
summer and sons,
her warm reprieves;
my meals, a home, and
grace.
this womb with a view.

you're not like them, she promises
me, herself,
corking the bottle,
bringing food, blankets,
a nourishing smile,
the smell of coffee and woman.

but I am sick again,
slouching toward Jotunheim—
a stranger,
goat-footed,
everything fierce:
the roads, streetlights,
and faces brutal.

at dawn, a soft touch
reels me back toward
cotton dreams
and plush repose—
hours into morning
days and days if lucky,
but
it's
just
a question of time.

PART FOUR

CODA

AFTERWORDS

When I first became aware of Clifford Meth by way of the Internet, he was, to me, simply this guy who always seems to be putting his dukes up at just the right moment. When something needed doing (while the message board posters were busy saying, "woe, oh, woe!" and "why is the world so unjust") Clifford always seemed to be the first guy to say, "Fuck that! Let's fix this shit!"

Dave Cockrum is unwell? Cliff didn't say, "Oh, that's so sad; he drew my favorite comic when I was twelve." No. It was, "Let's do a book! Let's do an auction! Let's go! Come on, get off your ass!" Gene Colan is ailing? "Let's sell stuff on Ebay! Let's get Marvel to help! Let's publish a tribute book!" And then he does it. And if you decide to be a doorstop or a doubter, well, get the hell out of the way, because you are no longer of interest. He doesn't care what you think of him, nor if you *know* it. There are things to do that actually *matter*.

I like that he is friends (or sadly *was* friends, in the case of Steve Gerber and Dave Cockrum, who passed away too damn early for me to believe in a just universe) with just the right guys, the men who believe "getting along" and "fitting in" aren't aspirations worth bothering about as an adult or an artist. Harlan Ellison. Gene Colan. Steve Gerber. Dave Cockrum. If you have these guys on speed dial, you're doing something very *right* in your life.

As for Gene Colan, man, what can I say about *that* guy?

When I was a little girl, I didn't care for the Marvel stuff. In fact, almost anything was preferable to the Marvel books in my young eyes. The art was too ugly and blocky, and lacked the slick clarity of the DC stuff. That lack of taste cost me dearly, because I missed out on reading those books as a kid, when they would have been the most mind-blowing. I missed out on Kirby, Ditko, and, sadly, Gene Colan.

But I made up for it later, rest assured.

It started with *Howard the Duck*, a book I had to buy no matter who the artist was, because I was, and remain, such a ridiculous Steve Gerber fan. But suddenly, trapped in another Gerber story of loss and desperation, I realized that this artist was unique, a visionary. While other artists excelled at character, this was the first comic I'd read where something new and grand was being reached for artistically: mood; a send of ominous dread, even in the funny moments. I had a feeling that this person saw the world differently than I did, and we were lucky that he had the talent to convey it.

I was an instant fan. I felt Gene was wasted on superhero books. Daredevil and the like were well drawn, of course, but I felt Gene came alive in the stories of rats and private detectives and Night Forces and vampires. He went on the very short list of artists whose work was an *instant purchase* and I always felt like I was getting the best end of the bargain. To this day, I'll often ask for a scene to convey dread or hopelessness or a foggy kind of moral ambivalence, and while I work with some spectacular artists, there's no question that Gene would know *exactly* what I wanted and deliver it in a way that quite possibly no one else in comics could.

Even in mainstream comics, we should bow politely and step aside when a visionary walks by. We should make room. Slick has its place. But vision can't be taught.

So, that's a lot of chatter about these guys and why I'm pre-disposed to like whatever they do. You can take my genuine pleasure at the pieces in this volume with a grain of salt, if you must, but I like this book. A lot. I read it in one gulp, and I expect to read it again. Probably more than once.

I like the certainty of Cliff's footing. The stories are whip-taut, with extraneous detail made simply unwelcome. There's a bit of an evil O'Henry in some of the stories, and the poems often manage to be painful and funny at once. Cliff writes about abusers and cads with the authority of one who might have seen some of that up close, but from which side of the fence, I have no idea. His stories start black and only get blacker. Somewhere on the label, there should be a warning: *This book is not approved for pansies.*

And Gene's pieces are wonderfully, if unsurprisingly, masterful and moving. It makes me mourn for the graphic novels the market hasn't allowed him to draw. In a just universe, he'd have drawn stories not just about Dracula and the Duck, but also about the people in this book—desperate, lonely people who have been kicked in the face and might be willing to dish some of that back. Bruised children, beautiful women glanced briefly from a distance, a man with a violin so lost in the music that he appears to be literally somewhere else...

Thankfully, we at least get the snapshots of those stories right here in this volume.

Thanks Cliff. Thanks Gene.

— Gail Simone
July, 2008
Nowheresville, Oregon

While this book features illustrations by Gene Colan, it's mostly Clifford Meth's work, and the most significant thing I can tell you about Cliff is that he asked me to make this afterword mostly about Gene Colan. That's altogether typical of the guy. Every single time I've crossed paths with Clifford, he's been en route to doing something caring and gracious for someone else, putting himself last so another can be first.

I was going to suggest that you can tell that from his writing, which is rich with passion and emotion and a deep understanding of what makes that oddest of all species, the putative human being, tick. But truth to tell, I do know other authors who write well and with like caring, but where they fall short is that they leave all that compassion on the page and muster little or none in their lives. Clifford is not among those authors. But he asked me to talk about Gene, not him, so…

Gene Colan is one of my favorite artists and has been since the day a new penciller named "Adam Austin" turned up in the pages of Marvel's comics. In the years that followed—under that pen name and later his real name—Gene produced so many fine pages that a lot of us took him for granted. We came to think it was the most natural thing in the world that comic art could look so good; that someone could so easily create Kirby-style energy in a comic but via a different, more photographic route.

Boy, did we not appreciate Gene! I mean, we appreciated him. How could you not appreciate him? We appreciated him on *Daredevil* and *Iron Man* and *Tomb of Dracula* and all the other books he drew, sometimes for long, uninterrupted stretches. But we didn't appreciate him nearly enough. Once he stopped producing two or three masterpieces per month, the whole comic rack just felt empty. Hollow. Something was missing.

Gene had that same sense of people. His Iron Man worked because he never lost track of the human being inside that clunky armor. You felt Tony Stark inside; you got a sense of his personality from the metal-encased body language and the ever-so-slightest variances in the helmet's facial expression. Gene made Daredevil and others gloriously real, as well. He even gave us a Dracula who was as human as he was inhuman.

AFTERWORDS

I met Gene at a 1970 comics convention in New York. Joe Sinnott introduced us and I was delighted to learn that, like Joe, another one of my favorite artists was a charming, friendly and humble individual. "Gentleman Gene" Stan Lee was calling him at the time… and Stan was never more correct.

In the last few years, Colan fans have emerged from everywhere. People who didn't even realize they were his fans suddenly had the revelation, realizing how much they missed his constant presence—how much they'd loved his work. The last few times I saw him and his lovely spouse Adrienne at conventions, I practically had to pole-vault over the masses just to say howdy. Which is great. And Gene is still the same lovely, way-too-modest guy he was when I first met him, which is also great. Thank you, Gene, for all you've given us.

And thank you, Cliff, for giving us a little more of Gene

— Mark Evanier
July 2008
Los Angeles California

"Scary Faces" is based on a short story that Gene Colan wrote decades ago and never quite finished. When Gene handed it off, Cliff managed to keep its characters and mood intact while twisting it in ways Gene would never have gone.

SCARY FACES

"Come, Will. There's nothing to be afraid of."

Will Chaney felt his mother's warm hand gave his own a gentle squeeze as she tried to reassure him, but her words were little comfort to the boy. The world can be a scary place for children. Sometimes it was even frightening for adults—his father admitted as much as he sat listening to the radio each night at eight o'clock sharp. Mark Chaney, a strong-chinned, broad-shouldered, barrel-chested immigrant who worked ten-hour shifts each day in the garment district to feed his family, a coarse man who responded to the outer world with a narrow cynicism, would park himself across from his demur wife at their tiny kitchen table, a sugar cube in his mouth, a glass of hot tea set before him on a tablecloth wiped clean of dinner crumbs by that obedient woman, and there he'd allow himself to become engrossed in the mesmerizing, erotically authoritative words of Walter Winchell. Yes, Will knew that his father was frightened, too. The monsters he called *krauts* had invaded Poland.

Poland. Even the name sounded exotic to young Will! *Poland.* Land of Po. The old country; the antiquated world that his parents had been born into and escaped. And now their birthplace, which still carried the romantic aftertaste of nostalgia, an occasional plague or sporting pogrom notwithstanding, now this Poland had been overrun by demons. They were horrible, these krauts, his father said. They were monsters. Will didn't have to try hard to imagine what they looked like. He'd seen the *Bride of Frankenstein* with his father at the pictures four years earlier. He imagined that krauts looked like the monster.

That afternoon, Will's mother brought him shopping. She'd bought him a Lime Rickey and gave him two pennies for licorice, but then she'd made him look at the display at the toy store. Hanging onto his mother's coat, panting like an overworked bellows, Will stood there clutching at his mother. "It's not real," she told him as his grip upon her tightened. *It's not real*, the words reverberating inside his head; *not real, not real…* But there they were—as real as anything… And they were staring at *him*! One had a huge bulbous nose and cracked teeth. Another had only one eye bugging out and spaghetti hair dripping down its face. *Krauts*, thought Will, knuckles whitening with tension as he gripped his mother's soft coat. *Krauts!* There was only glass between him and those horrible faces. He wanted to run, but desperately clung to his mother.

After what seemed like an eternity, Will's mother pulled him in another direction. How relieved he felt as they finally headed home, but he was still shaken by what he'd seen. Part of him wanted to hide. Part of him wondered if Walter Winchell had been to that toy store. His mother said they wouldn't see many more of those horrible faces as they walked down Coney Island Avenue but Will trembled at the possibility, block by block, as they neared their home. The clouds hung heavily in the sky and the wind whipped against the two while an occasional cluster of fall leaves whirled about them. Will finally began to relax as they neared his neighborhood, but he noticed there were other children outside, many wearing those horrible, scary faces. His mother hiked her collar up with one hand and pulled her son closer with the other. Once again, she tried to find just the right words to explain what Halloween was. "It's all make-believe, dear," she said. "All the children in Elmsford are just having a good time. Would you like to join Aunt Faye and her children tonight and go trick or treating?"

"No!" Will screamed. It was the first thing he'd said since they'd approached the toy store window. *No! No trick or treating! No more horrible faces! No!*

"But it's just *pretend*, dear."

"No! It's scary!"

Dorothy Chaney worried about her son. When he was younger, she'd allowed herself to believe that he might grow out of his *condition*. He'd been born smaller than other children and never quite caught up, not in height and certainly not in brains. Will was twelve now but he behaved like a six-year-old. Having a child like this put a constant strain on everything, not least of all her marriage. Mark blamed her for their child's problems, not that anything like this had ever occurred on *her* side of the family, but he was the type of man who couldn't blame himself for anything, let alone twisted eugenics. Neither was he the least bit accommodating. After Mark mounted that hideous shark's head in their bedroom, her son wouldn't even enter the room. "It's good he doesn't come in here no more," said Mark. "Now that you've popped your tittie out of his mouth, maybe *I* can get a turn."

Half a block before home, Dorothy Chaney saw the four neighborhood boys standing on the corner. Although she knew their mothers, she wasn't fond of these boys; in the past, they had been cruel to her child. Nevertheless, her husband had forbidden her interference. He said Will had to learn to stand up for himself, and part of her agreed. The other part suffered more than her child and was ready to lash out with her claws like an angry bear protecting its cub.

Will saw the boys, too. Each of them had on a scary face. All of them were familiar with Will's terror.

"There he is," said one boy. "Let's give him the business."

"Better not,' said another. "He's with his mother."

"Aw, so what? What can *she* do?"

The first boy, whose name was Kurt, swooped down toward Will and his mother. Kurt wore the most frightening mask that Will had ever seen—a death gray face carved by huge eye sockets with seemingly nothing behind them staring out; the mouth grinned from ear to ear with a lantern jaw and exaggerated teeth jutting outward. The boy caught Will's attention, riveting him to the spot. The sickly color of the mask, the absent eyes, the teeth—all of it bore down on young Will more horribly than the Frankenstein picture his father had taken him to.

"Hey, Will!" said the horrible face. "I'll take off my mask if you take off yours! Har-har!"

The other three boys laughed, too. Will tried to hide behind his mother, who was so beside herself that she didn't know what to do. She was about to scream, perhaps even slap the boy, when a single, solitary word brought everything and everyone to a startling halt.

"Krauts!" screamed Will.

There are certain words that end a conversation like the slamming of an iron door.

All of the masked boys stopped laughing. There was a moment of perfect, enduring silence, a vacuum through which the entire history of the species and all of its most hideous derivatives had license to pass. And then, chasing through that same chasm, the force that through the green fuse drove the species:

Spleen.

The boy in the death-gray mask, the one named Kurt, removed his horrible, frightening face only to reveal a more hideous one—the face of hatred, centuries old.

"What did you say, retart?" demanded the twelve-year-old. His eyes were flame. "You fucking Jew! You Christ killer!"

* * *

"It was horrible, Mark."

"It can be a lot *more* horrible."

"You didn't see their faces—you didn't hear what they said!"

"I've heard worse, believe me." Mark Chaney was unmoved. He'd ceased thinking of himself as Will's father but only as the overburdened husband of Will's mother. He'd ceased thinking of himself as a Polish Jew or an American Jew but only as a Jewish American, just like any other American. It was wishful thinking, but most thinking is wishful. "Be thankful you're in America," he said. "Here, it's *only* words." He snorted heavily. "Now make me a tea, wouldja? Winchell is on in a five minutes."

Dorothy Chaney poured hot water for her husband, then returned the kettle to the stove. "I'm going to look in on Will," she said.

"You'll miss Winchell."

"So I'll miss Winchell."

She wasn't surprised to find her child sitting up in bed. "Can't sleep darling?" she asked, sitting down beside him. Gently, she stroked his warm cheek.

Will looked at his mother with glazed eyes. "I want to sleep in your room," he said.

She smiled gently. "I think... it's better that you stay here."

"But I'm *scared*."

"There's nothing to be scared of."

"It's not pretend," he said.

Dorothy Chaney looked at her son. Oddly, it was as if she'd never laid eyes upon him before. There, in that brief moment, it dawned on her that her boy was emotionally smarter than anyone had given him credit for. His *condition!* *What* condition? *Every*one had a condition, she decided; some were just more insidious than others.

Will didn't say another word. His mother took him by the hand and led him out of the room.

Seeing them from the corner of his eye, Mark Chaney didn't look up from his radio program but raised a hand motioning his wife to be quiet. "Winchell is really giving it to those bastards..." When he glanced up, he noticed his son—his *wife's* son—standing there in his pajamas with pillow in hand.

"Where's *he* going?" Mark asked.

"To our bedroom," his wife answered.

"Like hell."

"It's necessary," she said, and with that she steered the boy by his shoulders under the threshold of her boudoir. It was his first time entering the room in years. The shark was still there, high on the wall, but what Will had seen and heard that day were worse.

"If he's in there where I'm ready to turn in," yelled Mark, "I'm sleeping somewhere else!"

"Suit yourself," his wife replied. A moment later she heard the front door slam. Apparently, that evening her husband would be missing Winchell as well.

* * *

Dorothy Chaney was sound asleep when Will heard the noise. He'd been determined to stay awake the entire night and had kept a faithful vigil. Instinctively, he knew he'd have to fight off anything or anyone attempting to enter and make off with him or his mother, anyone endeavoring to gobble them up or otherwise do them harm. The possibilities made him shiver beneath his thin blanket. He stared at the shark. It wasn't real, that shark, he thought. It had been real once but it had stopped being real. If it *were* real, Will realized, the shark would have eaten him.

Suddenly, he heard something. And then he heard it again. A scratching or a... No... it was something else... What *was* it?

The noise came from the front door. Will knew who it was. It was Frankenstein. It was the krauts. It was those boys who had called his mother a kike and a whore.

Will quietly crept out of bed. As frightened as he was, he moved with instinct and determination. He knew exactly what he had to do. He wasn't as stupid as they said he was.

Tiptoeing quietly, Will approached his mother's dresser then climbed up upon it and pulled the shark's head off the wall. It's huge teeth in that wide-open mouth looked even more terrifying up close. But it wasn't real. It wasn't pretend either. It was just *dangerous*.

In the kitchen, Will could hear quiet footsteps. He glanced over at his mother; she was sound asleep, breathing heavily through her mouth. He listened carefully. The footsteps were approaching the bedroom, coming toward them. Will positioned himself behind the bedroom door and raised the shark head as high as he could. Then, as the door opened, he brought the head down, teeth first, directly over the skull of the intruder.

Will heard his mother scream. And then she slowly approached them both, trembling uncontrollably as she cried.

She was still crying when the police came. Will noticed that the sun was already coming up. He liked the sun. Through the window, which his mother had cleaned the previous morning, he saw many of his neighbors standing about, staring and pointing at his house. Before the police took him away, he looked at the ground, gazed at the body lying in a pool of black-red blood that had already begun to congeal. He studied the broken head with several shark teeth punctured through its brow, one directly through the eye socket. It looked like one of the masks he'd seen in the toy store that morning, but not as scary.

A father's face is never *that* scary.

Economics 101

Hank was having another bad day compounded by the series of bad ones leading up to it; money problems mostly, women problems mostly, the black despair of middle age hanging on like a brutish wet animal; there was nothing to do with a beast so damp and stupid but embrace it and go for broke, buy it a drink, get it laid, and for christfuckingsake, stay away from firearms. The Argentinians had a word for it: *divaganda*. Maybe that wasn't it. But bifurcated as he was, Hank dialed the number of a Russian bitch who, once sprung, might kill several small birds with one stoning.

"Hello?"

"Helena—it's Hank."

"Oh, hello, Hank. I'm surprised you call. You're not mad that I stood you up the other night?"

"I was at the time but you told me it was an emergency."

"Yes. Emergency. My friend needed baby sitter for her daughter."

"Yes, you said that. I only waited half an hour then went home and watched the ballgame."

"I do not like baseball."

"That's too bad."

"It is not *too bad*."

"Look," he said, "let's make up for it tonight? I'll pick you up at 8:30. Take you anywhere you want to go."

"8:30," Helena repeated. She thought about it for a moment, weighed her options, or perhaps just pretended to. "Okay," she finally said.

Hank hung up and suddenly forgot all about his bad day. He'd been trying to get a date with Helena ever since he'd met her at the all-night laundry several weeks earlier. The thirty-year-old Russian was nearly as flat-chested as a fourteen-year-old, with the strong, thin, muscled legs of a ballerina. He thought about those legs as he quickly showered and changed his shirt then put on clean underpants and his best boots. Then he was out the door.

Helena lived alone in a garden apartment twelve miles west of Murryville. As he pulled up to the curb, Hank was imagining what the inside of her apartment looked like but Helena was already outside waiting, the front door locked behind her like the gates of Stalingrad before von Paulus's 6th army; she didn't give him a chance to get out of his car but walked up to the passenger side, opened the door and got in. "You didn't get lost?" she asked, offering Hank her hand to shake. Hank accepted the small, strong hand and gently kissed her knuckles, which smelled of lotion. "Already with the hand kissing?" she asked mockingly, all Soviet and superior.

Hank looked her over—she was less than 100 lbs., about 5'3" of taut, lean muscle, her small breasts protruding through her black leotard, her bare arms tight and defined, her strong, thin legs dangling from the tawny shorts she'd chosen, her hair twisted in a sloppy bun at the top of her head; she had high cheekbones and dark, intelligent eyes. Other than her military aspect, it was hard not to want to fuck her. Or perhaps because of it.

Ten minutes later, Hank pulled up at a neighborhood bar, parked out back, and the two walked into the joint. Helena surveyed the room, then chose a small table at the corner of the bar, deposited her small bottom on top of a stool, looked at herself in the tabletop mirror and said, without looking up, "Get me a Tezon Blanco. On the rocks with three limes."

"I thought you said you drink Tequila," said Hank.

"What do you think Tezon Blanco is? That is the *best* Tequila!" She wasn't kidding. A tumbler of the stuff cost Hank three times one of his beers. But what the hell, he thought—at 80-proof and her at 98 lbs., two shots should be all it took.

Hank was wrong again. Helena ordered a third Tezon Blanco, then a double for her fourth. The double cost him a twenty, a five, and two ones for a tip. He watched as she jabbed violently at the limes in her drink with the edge of a stirring straw, all the while going on and on about how stupid and ignorant Americans are. "You think it was all economics!" she said of détente, "but that is how stupid and ignorant Americans are!" She downed her drink. "You know," she said wiping her mouth on the back of her hand, "I married a stupid fucking American. I was very young at the time—what the fuck did I know? Young and in love! It lasted about a month. We're still good friends—he is very cool guy, very smart for American. Most Americans don't read, at least American *guys*, but he would read sometimes if I gave him to read something, and he was very smart about music. He played in a band, I don't remember what the fuck they were called. Something about flames. Flaming fucking something. But he would read sometimes. Americans don't read. They don't know Nabokov, except that one book. Or Pushkin! I read Pushkin as a girl in Soviet Union. My mother, who was genius, she made me take ballet lessons and gymnastics and she had many good books. I loved Pushkin the most. I also loved Oscar Wilde even more, but he was English, not Russian. A miserable guy."

"All of us are in the gutter," said Hank into his beer.

"Oscar Wilde was homosexual," she continued. "They put him on trial because of being homosexual, those crazy fucking British." At the rate she was sucking down Tezon Blancos, Hank couldn't afford another beer so he sipped at his warm one as Helena expounded upon the crazy fucking British before returning to the subject of stupid fucking Americans. "John Updike? Shit. And these Jewish writers? Roth and Bellows? Shit. The Russian writers were the best. You Americans don't read any of them—you don't read Americans either, I'm sure. You are too busy with baseball or Fourth of July or economics. You don't know the great Russian writers except maybe a little Tolstoy and Dostoevsky, and maybe a little Chekhov. But you don't know about Vladimir Mayakovsky or Boris Pasternak or Anna Akhmatova or Joseph Brodsky or Gorky or Sholokhov." She reached for her drink.

"You forgot Bulgakov," said Hank.

"What?"

"You forgot Mikhail Afanasievich Bulgakov." Hank finished the last drops of his warm beer. "His best work was *The Master and Margarita*."

"You read Bulgakov?" asked Helena, astounded.

"Not on purpose," said Hank. "I prefer Americans authors. American novels are essentially boy meets girl. French novels are boy meets girl, boy loses girl. Russian novels and boy meets girl, boy loses girl, and this takes 900 pages."

Helena ordered another Tezon Blanco. Hank looked in his wallet. He was already out a hundred bucks and wondered how many more Tezon Blanco's were necessary to pry Helena out of her tawny shorts. That's when Helena got sick. She looked like she'd swallowed bad paste and might hag at any moment. Hank suggested that they get some air, but she declined and ordered a big, greasy plate of nachos instead.

"I am too drunk for air," she finally said, wiping her mouth. "I need to eat."

"You just knocked off three pounds of nachos and cheese," said Hank. "What do you want now, a hamburger?"

"No—I'm okay," she decided. "Just take me home."

So Hank did. In her driveway, he leaned in for a kiss.

"Already with the kissing," said Helena in her mocking Soviet accent as she turned her cheek. Hank managed to get his arms around her for a few minutes, bury his face in her neck and fondle her small breasts before she squealed with delight, then pushed him away. "Listen!" she said, very Soviet—Hank realized that no matter what she was about to say in that accent, it would sound like an order, or the announcement before the big one was dropped. "*Listen*, I am on my period! Do you know what happens when a woman is on her period?"

"I have a vague notion," said Hank.

"It is like bloody nose," said Helena. "And alcohol only makes it worse. I am usually very sexual but not when I am on my period. Call me tomorrow." At which point Hank smiled politely and bid her adieu.

Twenty-three minutes later, he pulled up in front of the Shakin' Lady Lounge. He was already $128 in the hole for the night—figured he might as well throw good money after bad. He walked into the bar and looked around. Most of the women were fairly worn, some more than others, but one in particular stood out. Hank approached her and asked her name.

"Natalia," she said.

Her accent was familiar. "Where you from?" he asked.

"Ukraine," said the girl, adjusting her halter top.

Hank moved away from the bench. He looked around. The place hadn't changed a bit.

"Hey buddy," said a guy standing next to him. Hank turned and encountered what could have been his twin, except the guy was twenty years older and bald and fat. "What's the difference," the guy asked, "between a Russian girl and her mother?"

"I give up," said Hank.

"About twenty dollars," said the guy.

Hank moved toward the tables at the back of the room. That's where he sat down to contemplate his fate.

"Looking for someone?" asked another voice. It wasn't Russian.

Hank spun on his stool to find himself facing a dark-skinned girl. She looked Dominican. "I'm Michele," said the girl. "You want a dance?"

"What I want," said Hank, "is not to be teased any more. I'm having a bad day."

"You'll like the dance," said the dark girl taking him by the hand.

Hank bought two dance tickets for twenty dollars each. Then the two entered a private booth. Michele wasted no time. She dropped to her knees, unzipped his fly and went to work.

Six minutes later, Hank said, "Thanks."

"No problem," said Michele. She wiped him off. "I'm here every Thursday night. I don't think I've seen you here before."

Hank stood up and handed her a third twenty for a tip. "I never come here," he said.

"Never?"

"Only when I'm having a really bad day."

"Well, I hope your day gets better," said Michele.

"It will," said Hank, "if the Soviets don't drop the big one."

The following appeared as an Afterword in the second edition of Perverts, Pedophiles & Other Theologians, *published five years after the book's first printing.*

THE LAST WORD

If you're holding this book in your hands or your feet or your tentacles or somewhere else, you're one of the privileged few who purchased this second edition of *Perverts, Pedophiles & Other Theologians*. For that, I thank you.

Indeed, when the nice folks at Diamond Distribution informed Aardwolf Publishing that they wanted another print run of Perverts—a book that Gene Colan and I completed five years ago—I was particularly pleased. For one, it meant that a new audience was waiting, and that there'd be some more money in the kitty. It was also an opportunity to speak to you, gentle reader, for the first time in a painfully long stretch.

Yes, I said painful.

I don't believe in coincidences. I'll tell you what I do believe in some other time. Nevertheless, I find it almost eerie that in his generous introduction to this book, Steve Gerber addresses the notion of The Pain of Writing. Or, to be more precise, The Pain of Not Writing.

When *Perverts* was delivered to the publisher in the spring of 1997, I was only aware of that pain from a distance. I'd heard of it, anyway. Who hasn't? But in my mind's eye, writer's block was like Biblical leprosy. Frightening, yes, but hardly a clear and present danger.

Then it hit. Hard. Like a heavy bludgeon just below the ear.

It was a year to the month after *Perverts* had shipped—March 2, 1998, to be precise. 5:35 p.m. A Monday. I'd returned home from the office, pulled my Toyota into the driveway, and parked. I was feeling pretty good, as I recall, although it's hard to recall anything before that day without filtering it through the last four years of my life. I do distinctly remember turning the key in the lock, opening the front door, and calling out to my wife and children that I was home—a ritual I'd grown accustomed to and one that would, sadly, come to a full stop that day.

No one returned my greeting. My family was gone.

There was no note, no message on the answering machine—no sign of a break-in or other happenstance. Just an empty house that somehow felt abandoned.

It is every parent's worst nightmare. There are no words to describe this.

After several frantic hours of phone calls to friends, neighbors, and police, I finally pieced together my new reality.

I'd actually visited this nightmare several years earlier in a story entitled "The Promise" (published in *This Bastard Planet*, 1995). In that tale, a small boy is snatched from his father's home by his estranged mother and her boyfriend. Upon discovery of the crime, the father sets out on a holy mission, leaving no stone unturned in his desperate attempt to recover his child.

My reality was somewhat different, but only in the details. My wife was not estranged from me. At least, not as far as I knew prior to 5:35 p.m., March 2, 1998. Neither was there a supplementary man in the picture. At least, not as far as I knew prior to 5:35 p.m., March 2, 1998.

The details of that crisis are for another time. I'll just tell you the ending now: I got the kids back. Today, they all live with me. Being relentless has its advantages.

The wife, alas, never returned. The supplementary man, alas, is still discovering the munificent nuances of the word relentless. What goes around comes around.

As for The Pain of Not Writing, I'm sorry to report that I've suffered from it for years, now. But I've also learned to live with it. As some writer once observed, you can't have everything, and sometimes you can't have *anything*.

And sometimes you can.

— Clifford Meth
April 2002
Rockaway, New Jersey

ANOTHER LAST WORD
(as if the last one wasn't enough)

It's been six years since I broke a four-year silence, if we want to be dramatic about it, and began putting down the word again. Fortunately, I can only conjure those quiet years now, years without writing, as one does a nightmare that has faded into the surreal, but I still recall the inciting incident itself with the clarity of an epiphany, as well as the inability to write about it or anything else, and that's drama enough. What abject self-loathing to hate even the thoughts in one's head! Of course, it wasn't entirely like that. My brain was pickled by circumstances. The force that through the green fuse drives the poem sometimes drives recklessly and sometimes forgets how to drive, or wants to. Six years later, six creeping years, healing years in some respects, years that were nowhere near as prolific as I'd have liked but were, at very least, free of suicidal impulses, six years and two more children, and once again I am reporting from the front.

Put simply, here's where I am right now, and this is what it looks like from here.

I enjoy Clifford's company less frequently, but attempt to keep pace with him. He still drinks more than I do, tortures himself more exquisitely, curses with greater panache, appears on moon-lit nights outside my balcony beckoning me to journey with him to the heart of darkness and leave shrunken heads on tall spikes. And this, when all I want to do is stay home and read and sleep. Perchance to dream. On such nights, I can't help but question the differences between good citizenry and bad, between the reality of perception and the perception of reality, especially with regards to the ocean of lost souls I swim in. Just for fun let us journey, momentarily, to a drinking establishment for an example, where such a lost soul, a woman who once played classical piano at Moscow University and has now emigrated to the U.S. seeking *the good life,* finds herself suspended from a pole in front of two dozen pairs of tit-sucking eyes and using her breaks to give hand jobs (a.k.a. "lap dances") for twenty-dollar tips. Now I ask you: Is our gal any less of a pianist by dint of her current profession? Or any less of a hand-job artist for being able play Rachmaninoff's third piano concerto with the other five fingers?

The conundrum stalks me like one of Robert Bloch's fiends as I wrestle with my own angel, walking the fine lines of fatherhood and working stiff and good citizenry and sometimes not such good citizenry. For instance, after reading some of the introductory comments in this volume, I find it unfair not to note that any acts of perceived charity on my part are precariously balanced by fits of depression, a desire to be left alone, and infrequent acts of vengeance (which, in all fairness, I have elevated to an art form—and for good reason!)

Nothing has changed. And I am no less perplexed by my own dark side than I am by our concert pianist of two paragraphs prior. Will my two new children, to say nothing of the six-dozen others I may or may not have fathered, perceive me as a writer who fights, or a fighter who occasionally writes? More importantly, why is this the locus of how I spent my summer vacation? I'll tell you why: *Because it's damn unsettling seeing other people describe you in print.* If you're not careful, you might start to believe some of it.

More than anything else, I'm a victim of foolish consistencies. I have learned that your head can tell you one thing while your whole life tells you something else. And *that*, my friends, is the presiding thought that struggles to take the reins six years later as I attempt to cram into a fortune cookie yet another portion of a lifetime spent. At 47, I can only offer bumper stickers of mid-life sophistry. Here they are:

- Integrity is not negotiable.
- Perseverance pays off.
- You haven't lived until you've heard the words, "Come out with your hands where we can see them!"
- Not eating a bullet is usually the right choice.
- Vengeance almost always relieves indigestion.
- And the lamb will eventually lie down with the lion.
  But the lamb won't get much sleep.

   — Hank Magitz
   July 2008
   Murrayville, New Jersey